P9-CPX-614

THE
TIME
CAPSULE

You'll want to read these inspiring titles by

Lurlene McDaniel

One Last Wish novels
Mourning Song • A Time to Die
Mother, Help Me Live • Someone Dies, Someone Lives
Sixteen and Dying • Let Him Live
The Legacy: Making Wishes Come True • Please Don't Die
She Died Too Young • All the Days of Her Life
A Season for Goodbye • Reach for Tomorrow

The Dawn Rochelle novels
Six Months to Live • I Want to Live
So Much to Live For • No Time to Cry • To Live Again

Other fiction by Lurlene McDaniel
Garden of Angels
A Rose for Melinda
Telling Christina Goodbye
How Do I Love Thee: Three Stories
Angel of Mercy • Angel of Hope
Starry, Starry Night: Three Holiday Stories
The Girl Death Left Behind
Angels Watching Over Me
Lifted Up by Angels
Until Angels Close My Eyes
Till Death Do Us Part
For Better, for Worse, Forever
I'll Be Seeing You • Saving Jessica
Don't Die, My Love
Too Young to Die
Goodbye Doesn't Mean Forever
Somewhere Between Life and Death
Time to Let Go
Now I Lay Me Down to Sleep
When Happily Ever After Ends
Baby Alicia Is Dying

**From every ending
comes a new beginning. . . .**

Lurlene McDaniel

THE
TIME
CAPSULE

DELACORTE PRESS

Published by
Delacorte Press
an imprint of
Random House Children's Books
a division of Random House, Inc.
New York

Visit us on the Web! www.randomhouse.com/teens
Educators and librarians, for a variety of teaching tools, visit us at
www.randomhouse.com/teachers

Library of Congress Cataloging-in-Publication Data

McDaniel, Lurlene.
The time capsule / by Lurlene McDaniel.
p.   cm.
Summary: Reminded of what life was once like by the opening of a
first-grade time capsule, seventeen-year-old Alexis now faces the
pressures of senior year in high school, her parents' total focus on
work, and the recurrence of her twin brother's leukemia.
ISBN 0-553-57096-X (hardcover)—ISBN 0-553-13051-X
(library binding)
[1. Twins—Fiction.   2. Brothers and sisters—Fiction.
3. Leukemia—Fiction.   4. Family problems—Fiction.
5. High schools—Fiction.   6. Schools—Fiction.
7. Miami (Fla.)—Fiction.]   I. Title.
PZ7.M13997Ti   2003
[Fic]—dc21   2003002365

The text of this book is set in 11.5-point Goudy Old Style.

Printed in the United States of America

September 2003

10   9   8   7   6   5   4   3   2   1

This book is lovingly dedicated to my kid brother,
Jim Gallagher.

What good is it, my brothers, if a man claims to have faith but has no deeds? . . . . faith by itself, if it is not accompanied by action, is dead.

JAMES 2:14, 17 (NIV)

Dear Senior:

Hi there! It's me, Ms. Lola . . . from your first-grade classroom at Woodland Elementary School in North Miami. You remember me, don't you? Because I remember you as adorable children who passed through my classroom eleven years ago. I know, I know—you're wondering, "Gee, why is Ms. Lola writing to me after all this time?"

I'm writing because I want you to join me in a celebration picnic here at Woodland Elementary. First, I'm celebrating twenty-five years of teaching first grade. But more than that, I'm celebrating YOU, my students—that is, all of you I can locate who are still attending school in the greater Miami area!

Think back to your last day in my classroom. I asked each of you to write down what you wanted to be or do when you grew up. Remember how we put all the pieces of paper into a box I called the time capsule? Well, guess what? It's time to open the capsule and reread all those messages.

So please come to the picnic, get reacquainted with one another, eat pizza and cake and meet my

1

brand-new class of first graders. We'll meet outside under the giant banyan tree by the playground on the last Friday of August at 3:00 P.M.

Please come! The time capsule awaits!

With affection,

Mrs. Lola Tredayne
(aka Ms. Lola)

Woodland Elementary School

ONE

"The school looks exactly the same," Alexis Chappel told her brother, Adam. Together they walked from the parking lot across the grounds of their former elementary school, toward the huge banyan tree that sheltered the playground.

"I haven't thought about this place since we moved," Adam said. "Everything looks so small."

"That's because we're bigger," Alexis said. "And I used to think about it all the time. I really missed it when we moved." Their family had relocated to the southwest side of Miami during the summer following fourth grade, and twins Adam and Alexis had transferred into a brand-new elementary school. Alexis remembered how she had cried because she had loved Woodland Elementary, which was just around the corner from their old house. The low-slung building of

3

white stucco, yellow brick and awning-covered windows looked tired and dingy to her now, eight years later. "You think we'll recognize anybody?"

Adam grinned and pointed. "I recognize Ms. Lola."

Beneath the giant tree, Alexis saw a diminutive woman with a frizzy mass of red hair herding a group of children toward rows of benches. Behind the benches there were several rows of chairs where teens sat, some talking, some eating slices of pizza and sipping canned sodas.

"Is that our class?" Adam asked, pausing to check out the group.

"Did you expect everybody to be six?" Alexis teased. "The letter said our classmates would be invited." Adam was the shyer of the two, and Alexis usually felt as if she was either pushing him or dragging him to do something. But then, Adam's life had been a whole lot more difficult than hers.

Ms. Lola looked up, saw them and dashed over, her face lit with a smile. "I'm so glad to see you. My beautiful twins. Do you know that in all my years of teaching, I've only had three sets of twins in my classes? But you two were my favorite. I never had to worry about telling you apart!" She hugged them, and a jumble of warm, fond feelings flooded through Alexis. To this day, she'd never loved a teacher the way she had loved Ms. Lola. "You both look wonderful! Come, join the others," the teacher said. She led them to the rows of chairs and began to introduce them to eleven former classmates.

Alexis smiled and waved at each person, recognizing names because she had pored over their first-grade class photo and roster before coming. There had been twenty-eight in the class. Some she knew from the old photo, but others looked totally different.

"Grab yourself some goodies and have a seat," Ms. Lola said, then rushed off to greet a group heading across the playground.

"Want a soda?" Adam asked.

"Sure. I'll save you a spot."

Once Alexis had settled in, a girl two chairs over asked, "Remember me? Linda Cummings. I sat behind you in first and third grades."

"I remember." Alexis flashed her brightest smile. "You had long, curly brown hair."

Linda's hair was now short and was dyed pink and red. "And you wore a long braid that usually had ribbons going through it," she said. "I used to sit there and wonder what it would be like to have such pretty, straight black hair."

"It was monotonous. Nothing I did then or do now makes it curl."

Linda's gaze lingered on Alexis's long hair. Finally she shifted self-consciously and asked, "Where are you going to high school?"

"South Kendall. And you?"

"North Miami High."

"It seems weird to be back," Alexis confessed.

"I've lived in the same house since first grade." Linda sounded apologetic about it. "Ms. Lola had no trouble tracking me down. I couldn't stay away. I wanted to see how we all turned out. Plus, I want to know what's in that time capsule of hers. I don't remember writing anything. How about you?"

"I can't imagine what I wanted when I was in first grade. That was ages ago."

Linda glanced toward Adam, who was putting pizza on paper plates. "I don't remember what I wrote, but I remember what I wanted. I had the worst crush on your brother and wanted him to notice me. He's still cute."

"He's got a girlfriend."

"All the cute ones do," Linda said with a sigh. She added, "I used to envy the two of you."

"You're kidding. Why?"

"Because you got along really well together. My older sister and I fought like cats. I remember how you and Adam used to finish each other's sentences."

"We still do. It's because Adam and I were *womb* mates," Alexis said. Their peculiar link with each other was very real, and at times it seemed as if they could almost read each other's minds.

Linda grinned. "*Womb* mates—I get it. So who's older?"

"I am. By seven minutes."

"Are you and Adam in classes together?"

"No. He's into math and baseball. I like speech and debate."

"Debate. Isn't that when you argue with someone?"

"It's really problem-solving competitions. Teams get proposals or resolutions in advance and prepare arguments for and against them. It's fun." The competitions were tough, but Alexis loved the high that came when she scored enough points from the judges to advance to the next round. She was team captain and had racked up more points than anyone on her school team so far. Mrs. Wiley, the debate coach, was already prepping Alexis and the team for the state tournament to be held in Tallahassee, the state capital, in the spring.

"Do you want to be a lawyer?" Linda asked.

"Maybe." In truth, Alexis wanted very much to attend law school. She supposed the tendency for high achievement ran in their family. Their father, Blake, was an attorney, and their mother, Eleanor, was a top-selling real estate agent and a community activist interested in running for public office. "Ambitious parents create ambitious kids," Adam often said. "And one out of two isn't bad. With you, Ally, they're batting five hundred."

Adam returned, bringing Alexis a cold lemon-lime soda, her favorite, and a plateful of pizza slices. She introduced him to Linda, whose face took on a pink hue when Adam said hello.

"We were in the same class," Linda said, stating the obvious and blushing again.

"You want a soda?" Adam asked.

"Um, no thanks—I mean, sure, thanks."

He gave her a quizzical look. "What flavor?"

"Yellow. I—I mean, lemon-lime, like your sister's."

Adam left, and Linda groaned. "If he asks, tell him I don't get out much."

Alexis laughed. "It's okay. I'm sure he didn't notice a thing."

Adam returned with Linda's soda just as Ms. Lola went up to a podium under the tree, facing the rows of benches and chairs. The microphone, attached to a portable amp, screeched, and everyone covered their ears. "Oh dear," Ms. Lola said. "Oh, that's better," she added as the mike stabilized. She was dressed in green, and Alexis thought she resembled a storybook elf.

Adam leaned toward Alexis and whispered, "She looks like one of Santa's elves."

Alexis whispered, "You read my mind."

"I want to thank all of you for coming to today's time capsule ceremony," Ms. Lola said. "I do this for a couple of reasons. First, I want all of you to remember what your lives were like in first grade, now that you're seniors. I want you to remember the things that were important to you way back then."

Alexis heard kids shuffle all around her. On the benches where the current first graders were lined up like birds on telephone wires, she saw little heads turn to look them over. She ventured a wave and heard giggles.

"Another reason I like having this ceremony is to encourage these first graders. While you are here today for this ceremony, I'm sorry to say that four from your original class have dropped out of school altogether. That makes me sad." Ms. Lola looked downcast, then brightened. "But of the kids from your class still living in the Miami area, sixteen are here, all of you seniors, and all of whom, I hope, will be going on to college."

Ms. Lola continued. "Now, I know all of you are ready for more pizza and for that scrumptious cake that's waiting to be cut, but first I want to open the time capsule and read your papers. Is everyone ready?" Ms. Lola pulled a metal box from beneath the podium and raised the lid. She pulled out a thick manila envelope and looked up. "You see, I believe that when we're children, we're a whole lot closer to knowing our true hearts. As we grow up, real life can get in our way and set us on other paths. *Now* is the time to reconnect, to make changes. *Now*, before your official school days are over. *Now*, while you still have time to dream and plan." Ms. Lola paused, gazing out over the group. Alexis could swear the teacher had tears in her eyes.

Ms. Lola cleared her throat and opened the envelope. "I'll say your name and read your note; then please come up and get your paper. Take it home and post it where you can see it throughout this school year. Perhaps it will serve as a stepping-stone for your future."

Alexis and Adam exchanged knowing looks. After the pain and uncertainty of Adam's past several years, he deserved a bright future. Alexis longed to squeeze his hand for reassurance but knew that doing so would embarrass him. So she shifted forward in her chair and silently beamed him positive thoughts. *Of course it will, Adam.* And then, because she wanted it to be true so very much, she added, *Please, God. Let it be so.*

TWO

"What did you write down?" Sawyer Kennedy, Alexis's boyfriend, asked when she arrived home from the ceremony. He was waiting for her out back on the deck area by the pool.

Alexis plopped onto a lounge chair shaded by a colorful umbrella. "Something dumb," she groaned. "Can you believe I wrote *I want to help people?*"

"What's so dumb? I think it's nice."

"Puh-leeze. How vague is that?"

Sawyer looked bewildered. "What did your brother write?"

"That he wanted to be a fireman."

"What's so different?"

She unfolded the piece of wide-lined primary school paper and studied her neatly formed block letters. "At least being a fireman is a specific goal. What's *help people* mean?"

Sawyer grinned and tugged the paper gently from her fingers. "Do you want to be a fireman now too?"

"Adam picked something concrete and achievable, and I turned into a space cadet. What would you have written down?"

"That's easy. I wanted to be a professional soccer player. Or a sex god."

She rapped her knuckles lightly against his skull. "Speaking of concrete . . ." She'd been dating Sawyer since the middle of their junior year, and she liked him, but he wasn't deep or complicated, which sometimes frustrated her. She held out her hand. "My paper, please."

He grinned. "I'm holding it for ransom. Give me a kiss."

Usually she would have joked with him, but for reasons she herself didn't understand, she felt out of sorts and downright cranky. Even though she and Adam had hung around eating and visiting with their former classmates after the readings, the time capsule ceremony had left her depressed. "The paper, Sawyer."

He held it out of her reach. "Kiss first."

"Don't rip it. It's been saved since the first grade. Now, give it to me." Alexis knew her voice sounded sharp, but she couldn't help it.

Sawyer's expression turned apologetic, like a scolded child's. He stood, took a step forward, paused, then darted toward her, kissing her on the mouth before she had time to react. He placed the paper gently in her lap. "I was just teasing. Didn't mean to rile you."

Feeling ashamed, she refolded the paper. "And I didn't mean to snarl. Sorry."

He pulled her to her feet, stared deeply into her eyes. "It's okay. I got my kiss." His grin popped out like the sun peeking from behind dark clouds. "But then, I'm the fastest goalie in the county, so you shouldn't be too surprised."

Alexis returned his smile. It was difficult to stay miffed at him. Besides, he'd done nothing wrong. "But not the most humble," she teased.

"Don't need to be," he said. "My girlfriend keeps me humble. Why, a guy would have to have rocks in his head not to love her. Or maybe concrete."

She wound her arms around his neck. "Oh, hush up and kiss me again," she said.

After Sawyer left, Alexis cased the kitchen, only to find a note from their mother: *Your father's working late. I'm showing a client a house. Order pizza if you want.*

Alexis didn't want pizza, and not because that was what Ms. Lola had served at the picnic. She didn't want pizza because this made the fourth time in one week that her parents had been too busy to be home at dinnertime. The big house was eerily quiet. Like dark fingers, long shadows were creeping through the large bay window, across the polished terra-cotta tile floor and over the kitchen table. The glass surfaces gleamed, meaning that the housekeeper had been in that day. The table's centerpiece showcased plump glass and ceramic fruit in a massive pottery bowl. *Not even the fruit's real*, Alexis thought. She balled up the note and heaved it into a trash basket.

She became aware of a muffled but steady thumping sound. She knew just where it was coming from and went up the back staircase and down the hallway. She knocked on Adam's bedroom door.

"Enter," he said.

She did and found him stretched across his bed, his head propped on his book bag. He was tossing a baseball against the wall behind the door and catching it in his glove, something he did when he was either bored or deep in thought. She saw faint marks on the stucco wall behind the door where the ball had hit over and over throughout the years. "Mom and Dad won't be home until late," she said.

"I read the note."

"I don't want pizza. How about you?"

"I'll have a bowl of cereal later."

"I can fix us some soup."

"Don't worry about it. I'm not hungry."

Alexis shoved a pile of Adam's clothes onto the floor from his desk chair and straddled it. "I can't remember the last time we all sat down and ate a meal together," she said. "It's kind of funny, don't you think? Usually families don't eat together because the kids are too busy. But for us, it's our parents who are never home."

Adam rolled onto his side and raised himself up on his elbow. "Maybe they're avoiding us."

"Be serious. Doesn't it bother you? Even a little?"

"I ate a lot of hospital food by myself over the years, so no, I don't need company to chow down. Besides, I'd rather eat alone than sit through one of their frosty silences at mealtime."

Alexis rested her chin on the top of the chair. "They don't seem to have much to say to each other these days." The admission squeezed her heart.

"Unless they're fighting," Adam said. "Then they say plenty. At least they're not fighting about me anymore. That's a relief."

"You can't help what happened to you, Adam. You didn't ask to get sick."

"But I did get sick. And all those weeks and months of being in and out of hospitals over the years—well, it took its toll on them, and you know it. Took a toll on you too."

"I got over it."

"Did you get over Ms. Lola's time capsule event? You were pretty quiet on the ride home." Adam changed the subject, and Alexis knew he was finished discussing their parents.

She shrugged. "I guess. I was disappointed in my answer."

"Jeez, Ally, cut yourself some slack. You were six."

"That's what Sawyer said," she told him sheepishly. "Do you still want to be a fireman?"

"I'd rather be a famous baseball player, but I'll be a fireman, an astronaut, a rock star—any or all of the above. Most of all, I just want to graduate in June. I mean, turning seventeen in July was a big event for me. For *us.*" He tugged on a hank of her hair. "My doctors never thought I'd live past fourteen, remember?"

"But you did, and you'll live to graduate from high school and graduate from college and become whatever you want to become, because . . . because . . . well, because I say so!"

He laughed, ruffling her hair until she swatted his hand. "Your optimism keeps me going. You have enough willpower for both of us, you know." He bent, scooped a shirt off the floor and changed into it.

"Are you leaving?"

"I'm going to see Kelly. She'll have finished dinner by now, and maybe we can snuggle with a few books. I have a paper due for history next Friday."

Kelly Nielson was a pretty blond sophomore at their school. Adam had met her during the summer, and they had begun dating. Alexis thought the girl was ditzy and immature. "I predict you'll get more snuggle time than study time."

"That's my plan. You should call Sawyer to come back and keep you company."

"I'll wing it alone. I've got plenty to do. Big debate coming up, and I need to surf for information on the subject." Alexis's bad mood clung to her like a second skin. No use subjecting Sawyer to it.

"Your choice," Adam said, then picked up the car keys and left.

Minutes later, she heard him back the car they shared out of the garage and peel off into the night. Alexis went to her own room and opened her book bag. She shuffled through her stack of books, laid them out according to her class schedule and turned on her desk lamp and computer. The house was quiet once more, and with Adam gone, her mood turned melancholy. Was Adam right? Had his illness damaged their parents' marriage? Alexis thought of the weeks on end when their mother had stayed at the hospital with Adam while Alexis and their father fended for themselves. Certainly there had been a succession of housekeepers and professional caregivers to help out, but Blake had just made partner at the firm when Adam's illness had struck. He had kept long hours at his office, sometimes spending whole nights away from the house while Alexis longed for both her parents and cried herself to sleep.

Alexis still remembered her mother's absences and her father's stoic silences, peppered with occasional outbursts to doctors over the phone about Adam's treatments. She remembered visiting Adam's room and hospital floor, where she saw frail, sick children hooked to IVs and monitors and smelled the unmistakable odors of medicine and pine cleaners. She remembered wanting her mother to hold her and craving her father's reassurances. And she remembered fear. The fear that Adam would never return home.

She also remembered the years before Adam had gotten sick, of camping trips and family outings. Alexis plucked her favorite family photo from the bulletin board behind her desk, the one where her whole family was wearing Mickey Mouse ears and mugging for the camera. When she and Adam were nine, they had gone to Disney World. She recalled her parents stealing kisses in the dark tunnels of children's rides. "Gross!" Adam had pronounced.

A lump wedged in her throat. Her gaze drifted to her calendar, and suddenly she understood why the time capsule ceremony that afternoon had upset her. She missed those days. And she missed those parents. Everything had changed with their move across Miami, when she and Adam had been eleven and Adam had been diagnosed with a rare and virulent form of leukemia. Most victims had a brief yet fatal struggle. So far, Adam had beaten the odds. He'd been in a second remission for three years, but their family's lives had changed forever.

Alexis put the photo back in its place. It wasn't Adam's fault. It wasn't anybody's fault. If only she could put all their lives into a time capsule from before fifth grade, when Adam had been well and her parents had been happy. If only.

THREE

"Hey, Ally, wait for us."

Alexis turned at the sound of her name in the crowded school cafeteria to see her friends Glory, Tessa and Charmaine coming toward her. "What's up?" she asked.

"Thought we could eat together," Glory said.

"Where have you been?" Tessa demanded. "I called you yesterday afternoon to ask you to run to the mall with me and got your answering machine three times."

The girls set down their trays on a table.

"Adam and I went to this picnic and ceremony at our old elementary school. Special invitation by our former first-grade teacher."

Charmaine made a face. "Ugh! I'd never go back to my old school. I hated it."

"It was fun. Sort of," Alexis said. She

22

explained about the ceremony without mentioning the bleak mood she'd experienced afterward. They would never understand.

"Any cute guys?" Glory asked.

"And why would she be looking at other guys when she's got Sawyer at her beck and call?" Tessa asked.

"Never hurts to look," Glory said. She took a drink of her soda.

"You and Sawyer going to the game Thursday night?" Charmaine asked.

"Could Sawyer ever miss a sporting event?" Alexis wasn't crazy about football, but Sawyer had friends who played both soccer and football, so he attended every match, and because she was his girlfriend, she went with him. She added, "Besides, this is our final year to rah-rah the home team."

"Maybe we can sit together," Tessa ventured. "Will Adam be going?"

"Give it up, girl," Glory said. "Adam's only got eyes for that Kelly bimbo."

"Not nice," Charmaine said, wagging her finger at Glory.

"What's she got besides blond hair, blue eyes and a killer figure?" Tessa asked, blowing a puff of air that lifted her bangs off her forehead.

"Adam," Glory and Charmaine said in unison.

Alexis giggled. She liked Tessa especially. They were on the debate team together. While Tessa wasn't gorgeous, she was smart, with a caring, open personality. She'd had a crush on Adam for years, and Alexis often wished her brother appreciated Tessa's finer qualities. Alexis said, "I'm sure he's taking Kelly, Tess. Sorry."

"A girl can dream." Tessa gave a so-what shrug, but Alexis saw disappointment in her eyes.

"By the way," Glory said, "I signed us up for the Halloween Carnival committee."

"What? Without checking with us first?" Charmaine asked.

"I'm not sure—" Alexis started.

Glory waved them off. "Hey, sisters, we talked about doing this last year."

"How can you remember so far back?" Tessa asked. "Especially when you can't remember the six bucks you owe me from last Saturday."

Alexis half listened to their bickering. Halloween fell on a Friday that was also the end of a grading period, and there would be no school. The upcoming three-day vacation had given her an idea about how to bring her family closer together again. "I'll help," she said, interrupting her three friends. "My family may be out of town the weekend of the carnival, but I don't mind being on the committee to help plan it."

"Count me in too, then," Tessa said.

"Oh, all right," Charmaine grumbled. "Me too. But next time ask before volunteering us." She jabbed her fork into her salad.

Her friends kept talking, but Alexis tuned them out. She wasn't interested in the committee or the carnival. She was focusing on how to recapture the past.

"We're getting killed." Sawyer said, grimacing when their team's quarterback was tackled behind the line of scrimmage.

"The worst team in four years," Adam said.

"Hey, let's give them some support." This from Kelly, wedged between Sawyer and Adam on the bleachers.

Alexis, sitting on the other side of Sawyer, was already bored with the game in its second quarter. "We're ranked fifth out of five in our division, Kelly," Alexis said. "I don't think our team will turn it around."

All turned to look at her. "Where did you hear that?" Sawyer asked.

"The newspaper. A great source of information."

"Well, we're ranked first in soccer," Sawyer said. "Good thing too. Lots of scouts will be out eyeballing us, and I need a scholarship."

"I *love* soccer," Kelly said with enthusiasm. "It's my favorite sport."

"Do you play?" Alexis asked.

"Well . . . , no. But my kid brother does and I go to all his games, so I know all about it." She craned her neck, then pointed at the fence fronting the field. "Oh, look! There's Melanie Rodriguez. I bet she'll be voted homecoming queen this year. I know *I'm* voting for her. Are you?"

Alexis bit back a retort. For the life of her, she couldn't understand what Adam saw in this girl. She acted and talked as if there were only air between her ears. "Probably" was all Alexis could manage.

Just then Adam stood. "Come on, Kelly, let's beat the crowds and get in the food line before halftime." He started past Sawyer, Kelly behind him. "Want anything?"

"*Nada,*" Sawyer said.

"Me either," Alexis said.

As Adam passed her, he leaned down and in a low voice said, "Cut her some slack, Ally. She's only fifteen."

Alexis felt her cheeks flame. She should have known that Adam would be able to read her impatience with Kelly. "Sorry," she mumbled.

"Sorry about what?" Sawyer asked once Adam and Kelly were weaving their way down the stands full of people.

"Sorry that I'm judgmental and petty."

"Huh?"

She patted Sawyer's knee. "It's a long story."

He ducked his head, and she knew he wasn't going to ask her questions. It was just as well. She didn't want to talk about what was causing her ill humor. It really wasn't all Kelly. For days she'd been unable to corner either of her parents. Her father had worked late every night, and her mother had either been on her way to meet a client or working behind the scenes on a friend's campaign in the upcoming elections. How could she persuade them to do something as a family if they were never home long enough for her to talk to them?

"Hi. Why so glum?" Tessa sat beside her, waving to Sawyer as she did.

"Where are the others?" Alexis asked.

"Bathroom. I saw you all and thought I'd pop over. Crummy game, isn't it?"

"Worse than crummy."

The whistle blew on the field, signaling the end of the half, and the players streamed toward the locker room.

"I'm going down to talk to some of the guys," Sawyer said, leaving Alexis and Tessa alone. Students stepped around them in the exodus to the refreshment stands.

"You know, Tessa, I am so ready to be out of high school."

"Who isn't? Do you think college will be better?"

"It has to be."

Both girls planned to go away to college. Tessa wanted to attend the University of South Florida in Tampa, while Alexis hoped to be admitted to Stetson, a smaller, private university near Orlando.

"So what brought on this disdain for high school? Especially now that we're at the top of the heap?" Tessa asked.

Alexis glanced around. "It just seems there should be better things to think about than who's going to win a football game or who's going to be homecoming queen."

"Oh, I don't know. Innocence is a wonderful thing."

"How about ignorance? Is that wonderful too?"

"No way. One is a gift, the other is an act of will." Tessa leaned toward Alexis. "What are we talking about, anyway?"

Alexis burst out laughing. "I think my brother should be with you and not Kelly."

"Gee, what a coincidence, so do I." Tessa grinned, shook her head. "But the race doesn't always go to the fastest. I'm a realist, Alexis."

"And what am I?"

Tessa regarded her closely and pursed her lips, as if weighing her words. "I think you're a fixer, Ally. A person who tries hard to make everything right and everybody happy."

Tessa's assessment stung Alexis because it wasn't what she'd expected to hear. "What's wrong with that?"

"It sets you up for heartbreak. Sometimes things can't be fixed."

"Everything can be fixed, given enough time," Alexis countered. "That's what law is all about."

"No, law is about justice, remember?"

Alexis felt her face grow warm. "Of course. Good thing we're on the same debate team."

"Which reminds me, do you have your position paper ready for class? We go up against South Miami in two weeks."

"I'll be ready," Alexis said.

Tessa looked surprised. "Let me mark this day on my calendar. You're usually sitting around twiddling your thumbs while the rest of us slave away at the last minute. What's the holdup?"

"No holdup. I've just got other stuff on my mind."

Before Tessa could ask another question, Adam, Kelly and Sawyer returned.

"Hey, Tess," Adam said. He introduced Kelly, who waved and offered a bright, sparkling smile.

"Gotta run," Tessa said, standing abruptly and hurrying back up the bleachers.

"I don't think she likes me," Kelly said to Adam as Tessa climbed upward. "She didn't even say hello."

Adam slipped his arm around Kelly's shoulders. "Maybe she was in a hurry."

Feeling a need to defend her friend, Alexis said, "Tessa's about the nicest person I know. She would never snub anybody."

"Okay," Kelly said. "If you say so."

The referee blew his whistle, and the football game resumed. Sawyer reached for Alexis's hand, but she pulled away. She didn't feel like holding hands. If Sawyer noticed, he didn't let on. Alexis tuned out the noise of the crowd and turned her mind toward her plan to reunite her family.

FOUR

Alexis set her alarm clock for seven on Saturday morning. She groaned when it startled her awake, but she remembered why she'd set it so early and scooted out of bed. She slipped on shorts and a T-shirt, threw water on her face in her bathroom, tied her hair into a ponytail and hurried down the back staircase and into the kitchen. She found her father reading the paper and drinking coffee. "Morning," she said brightly.

Looking surprised, he said, "Morning to you. Why are you up this early?"

Alexis went to the refrigerator and poured herself a glass of orange juice. "No special reason."

"This *is* Saturday, isn't it?"

"All day." She carried her glass to the table and sat across from him. "Mom still asleep?"

He grunted. "Naturally."

"Want me to fry you an egg?"

"No. I have an eight o'clock tee-off at the club. I'll get something at the drive-through on the way."

It was his habit to play golf on the weekends, and he was always gone by the time the rest of the family got up. Alexis remembered that years before, her mother had fixed Saturday-morning breakfasts of bacon, eggs and toast that they'd eaten together at the table. On Sundays, she had fixed waffles. But no more. Now everybody went their separate ways on weekends.

"Do you know what the month of October is, Dad?" Alexis asked. She sipped her juice, hoping to cool her nervous, tight throat.

"Uh—October?" He didn't glance up from the paper.

"Okay, I'll tell you. October is Florida resident month at all our state attractions." He didn't respond. "It's when attendance is lowest at state attractions, and people who live here can get in for cheaper rates. It's been in TV ads."

"I don't watch much TV."

Alexis set down her glass and placed her hand on top of the paper, making him look up. "I have an idea," she said. "Want to hear it?"

"What?" His brow knitted.

She took a deep breath. "I was thinking that since it's a good deal to visit places in Florida, our family could take a few days and go to Disney World. You know, like we did when Adam and I were little. Low crowds. Low price." She held her hands up as if balancing a scale. "Adam and I have a three-day weekend coming up at the end of October, at Halloween, and so I thought it would be nice to take a family vacation. . . ."

"I don't see how I can do that. Too busy." His brusque tone only made her more determined.

"How can you say no? Halloween is still weeks away. Maybe you won't be so busy then."

He gave up on the paper and looked her in the eyes. "Honey, the firm's got more work than we can handle right now. I can't just pick up and take off."

"Friday, Saturday, Sunday. Three days, Dad. You'll miss one day of work and two golf matches. What's so hard about that?"

"Orlando's a five-hour drive."

"So we'll leave bright and early."

He cocked his head. "You're serious, aren't you?"

"Yes. We never go anywhere as a family anymore. And next year Adam and I'll be off to college, and you'll miss us horribly and say, 'Gee, I wish I could take my kids to Disney World,' but too late, we'll be gone."

He grinned. "You have great style, counselor. Did I ever tell you that?"

"Many times," she said smoothly, determined to keep the conversation focused. "Don't change the subject. Can we go to Disney World next month?"

"You and Adam go. Take a few of your friends. My treat." He picked up the paper.

She pulled it down again. "No, I want *us* to go. As in just our family."

He looked bemused. "You're a little old for Mickey Mouse, aren't you?"

"I'm still a child at heart." Her heart was hammering faster, just as it did when she knew she was arguing a position well during a formal debate.

Her father eyed the kitchen wall clock and stood. "I've got to run, Ally."

She dogged him to the back door. "I need an answer, Dad."

"You said we've got weeks to think about it."

"No, we've got weeks until we can go. We need to plan it now."

He turned, jingled his car keys. "Is it that important to you, honey?"

"Yes, it is."

Their gazes locked. "Tell you what. Line it up with your mother, and I'll clear my schedule."

"Oh, Daddy, thanks." She hugged him.

He kissed the tip of her nose, started out the door, turned. "Just make me a promise. Only one time around on It's a Small World, okay? It took me weeks to get that darn song out of my head the last time we went."

"Fair enough." She watched him hustle toward his Mercedes parked in the driveway. All smiles, she latched the door and crossed the cool tile floor, heading toward the staircase and her room. "One down, one to go," she announced to the quiet, immaculate kitchen.

"You can't be serious, Alexis."

"But I am serious, Mom." Alexis was beginning to feel exasperated. Her mother was proving a whole lot more difficult to convince than her father.

They were in Eleanor's home office, later that afternoon. Alexis had laid out her plan in clever, cute phrases, she thought, but her mother kept shuffling and piling papers the whole time Alexis talked. The desktop was covered with political posters and flyers.

"Halloween is a week away from the primary, Ally. And I am Larry Pressman's media coordinator. I can't take off a week before the election and go to Disney World. What are you thinking?"

"I am thinking that we haven't had a family vacation in years. And that this would be a good time to have one."

"Well, it isn't." Her mother ceased the paper diversion and, putting her hands on her hips, gave Alexis a pained look. "You know how hard I've worked on Larry's campaign. He needs me."

"What about us?"

Eleanor waved her off. "Don't sound so dramatic. It's not as if anybody here is neglected. There's food on the table every night, clean clothes in your drawers—"

"There's takeout most nights, and the housekeeper does the laundry."

"Well, excuse me, little Miss Ingrate. Let me chain myself to the kitchen sink and start sorting through my recipe box."

Nothing was going the way Alexis had planned it. "I didn't mean it that way. I'm not asking you to return to kitchen duty and give up your plans. I'm only asking for three days to come to Disney World with us. Dad's clearing his schedule. Why won't you?"

"Stop." Her mother threw up her hands. "I don't want to argue. Frankly, I'm too busy to argue. My working on Larry's campaign isn't just for fun, you know. If he's elected, he'll be very helpful to me this time next year when I run for city council. And I am going to run, Alexis."

"I want you to run," Alexis said, forcing her tone to be more placating, less adversarial. "Next year Adam and I'll be gone. You can run for president. But this year, all I'm asking for is one little three-day vacation together."

Her mother pursed her lips. "What is this really about, Ally? Vacation-taking time was last summer. You didn't say a word then."

"Dad had that big case and barely came home except to shower and change. You went off to that realtor convention in Dallas. There wasn't any time last summer either."

"So again I ask, what's this about?"

Alexis opened her mouth to speak, but the phone rang.

"Just a minute," her mother said, and picked up the receiver. The next instant, her face lit up. "Larry! How good to hear from you. I've got a list of things to go over with you. Are you free to meet this morning?"

Alexis shifted to catch her mother's attention. Her mother mouthed, *Later*, and started gathering paperwork with her free hand, all the while keeping up a stream of chatter to Larry Pressman. Alexis felt as if she'd been physically shoved aside. Anger bubbled, so she left the room before it could boil over.

She retreated to her bedroom, slamming the door with such force that pictures hanging on the walls shook. She stormed to her desk, jerked the photo of her family at Disney World off the bulletin board, ripped it in half and threw it in the trash. Then she started tossing clothes from dresser drawers.

"Did your ceiling fall in?" Adam had cracked her door enough to poke his head into the room. "I heard a racket."

"I'm cleaning drawers and closets," she said tersely.

"Need help?"

"No."

He came into her room anyway. "All right, sis, what set you off?"

"Nothing." She stopped suddenly, a wad of clothing in her hands. "Everything." Like a gust of hot wind, the fight went out of her, and tears brimmed in her eyes.

"Tell me." Adam sat on the corner of her unmade bed.

She told him about her conversations with their mom and dad. She finished her story by saying, "She just blew me off, Adam. It was like Larry's important and I'm nothing, an annoyance, like a housefly."

"I'm not too surprised." Adam leaned across her bed, pulled a tissue from the box on her bedside table and handed it to her. "You always could wrap Dad around your finger. He'd have agreed to anything. But when it came time to go, well, that would be different."

She blew her nose, glanced sidelong at Adam. "You think?"

"I'm positive. And so long as we're talking about it, did you ask me? What makes you think I want to go to Disney with them? I've outgrown Disney."

Alexis shrugged. "You're right. I should have asked you before going to them. I can't do anything right around here."

He leaned back on his elbows. "On the other hand, I might not be opposed to taking Dad up on his offer for you and me to take a few of our friends while he foots the bill."

"But you said you weren't interested in Disney."

"Not with the feuding Chappels. But you, me, Sawyer, Kelly—now, that sounds okay."

Alexis weighed the idea. "Kelly and I could share a room."

"I'm sure that's the only way her parents would let her go."

Alexis considered his suggestion. She wouldn't love being with Kelly, but since Adam liked the girl, she'd do it. "Do you think her parents will believe the sleeping arrangements? Better plan on taking a few others too. Safety in numbers."

"How about Wade?" He named one of his longtime friends. "And maybe Tessa."

"You'd like Tessa to come?"

"She's pretty easygoing. I'll be with Kelly anyway, so ask any of your friends."

"That leaves Tessa with Wade. They might think we're trying to force them together, and I don't think either of them would like that. They don't even know each other that well."

"We're not asking them to get engaged. They

can manage for a couple of days, don't you think?"

The more Alexis thought about it, the more she liked the plan. Adam was right. Who needed their deadbeat parents ruining a fun weekend because neither of them wanted to be there? "Let's do it," Alexis told her brother. "You set it up with Kelly and her parents and Wade. I'll get Tessa and Sawyer to commit." She paused. "And I'll get the money from Dad too. I'm sure he'll be thrilled to buy his way out of a family vacation."

FIVE

The thing that saved high school for Alexis was the work. She loved learning and classes that challenged her to think. Advanced Speech and Debate III and political science were her favorites, as were their teachers, Mrs. Wiley and Mr. Hernandez. Plus, Tessa was enrolled in those classes with her, making preparations for debate tournaments even more interesting. As a duo and with their team, they had won several trophies for their school, and Mrs. Wiley was certain the team had a shot at a state title at the Tallahassee tournament.

Alexis's specialty was original oratory, a wholly original speech that could last no longer than ten minutes and had to be presented without the use of notes or visual aids before a panel

of judges. If she won at state, it would look especially good on her application to Stetson.

"I've got to do something to stand out in the
pile of freshmen applications," Alexis told Tessa.
They were in the library, studying.

"Of course you'll stand out," Tessa said.

"I'm worried about the SATs. The math part,
you know? I've heard that Stetson won't even
consider students who don't score fourteen hundred or above."

"Oh, Alexis, really," Tessa said dismissively. "I
don't think qualifying for Stetson will be a problem for you."

Alexis shuffled her array of books. "Never
take anything for granted."

"What about Adam? Where's he planning to
go?"

"Probably Miami Dade Community for the
first year."

"You mean the inseparable twins are going to
be separated? I don't believe it."

"He thinks he's got a better chance of playing
baseball as a walk-on. Plus, his doctors want him
close by."

Tessa was one of the few people who knew
Adam's full medical history. His hospitalizations
had occurred when he'd been in elementary and

middle school; therefore, it was easy to *not* talk about it in high school. The student body was so large that Adam and Alexis seldom ran into kids from their old schools, and if they did, few remembered that Adam had even been sick. "And don't remind me that we'll be separated. I don't like thinking about it."

"It has to happen sometime. You have separate lives."

"I know, but it's not easy. When he hurts, I feel it. When I'm mad or upset, he knows it. It's like our brains are linked."

"Isn't that considered psychosomatic?"

"No, psychosomatic things are all in your head." She doodled as she talked. "It's more like telepathy."

"Doo-doo-doo-doo," Tessa joked. "How very *Twilight Zone*."

"Forget it," Alexis said, then changed the subject. "Are you okay about hanging with Wade when we go to Disney World?"

Tessa sighed. "Just so long as he knows I'm coming along to keep up appearances. Which, by the way, is kind of weird. Here's good old Tessa helping out so that Kelly's parents will be comfortable with their little darling going off with her boyfriend—who, coincidentally, is the one male on planet Earth that good old Tessa likes. Do you see any irony in this, Alexis?"

Alexis smiled and doodled Tessa's and Adam's names on her paper and drew a heart around it. "Yes, you are a good sport, girlfriend. And Wade knows you're not lusting after him."

"And Adam knows nothing about my stupid crush either?"

"Adam's clueless."

Tessa picked up her pencil, poised it over the doodle. "No need for him to ever know, okay? You keep that info inside your brain, Alexis Chappel. I don't want any telepathy leaking out my little secret. You hear?"

"Your secret's safe with me."

Tessa drew a jagged line between her name and Adam's. "No use wishing for what I can't have," she said with a shrug.

Alexis felt sad for her all over again.

South Kendall High took top honors in the first high school debate of the season. "Of course, it's not football," Alexis told Adam that evening as soon as she arrived home. "So it won't make the city papers." The house was empty, but she found him doing laps in the pool.

Adam pulled himself out of the water. "I'm

proud of you, sis." He shook water on her, and she jumped back.

"Hey! Don't get me wet."

He stretched out on a lounge chair. "Be glad you had something to do and you missed the fireworks."

"What fireworks?" She sat in the lounger beside his.

"The screaming Chappels. I came home from dropping off Kelly, and Mom and Dad were in a shouting match."

"Really?" The news made her heart hammer. "What about?"

"Dad's mad because Mom's spending so much time on the Pressman campaign. They were in her office, but I could hear them yelling through the closed door."

"Well, it's not like *he's* ever around," Alexis said.

"Exactly what Mom said." Adam reached for a towel. He dried his hair and pulled on a T-shirt. The sun had just gone down, and the air had turned cooler and less humid. "But I can't really blame him. Just me and you living here these days. She's always doing something for Larry. We're shadows."

"That's not true," Alexis said, then realized

that she agreed with her brother. "I—I think things will be better when the election's over."

"What if Pressman wins?"

"Mom will be happy."

"Maybe, but I heard Mom tell Dad that if Larry wins, he'll appoint her to some position on his staff. A reward, I guess, for her loyalty."

"What are you thinking?" Her heartbeat accelerated, because she knew what he was thinking, and she didn't want to think it—and neither should he.

Adam gave her a long look. "I'm thinking we should go inside and leave our parents to work out things on their own."

Alexis agreed. "I guess they both took off. When I came through the house, it seemed empty."

"I went to my room after the blowup, but I still heard some door slamming. They drove off in separate cars around five."

The news depressed her. "I ate with Tessa on the way home from the tournament, so I'm not hungry. If you want, I'll heat up some macaroni and cheese for you."

"I'm not hungry."

"You should eat."

"I had a burger with Kelly on the way home from school."

"Good. We need our strength for Disney World."

"Is the trip all set?" Adam started toward the house, and Alexis followed.

"Dad said he'd give me his credit card and said for us to have a good time."

"Sounds great to me."

The lights from the patio and pool made circles on the concrete. Alexis squinted. "Is that a bruise on the back of your leg?"

He glanced down. "Just shadows."

"Let me see."

Adam turned away, twisted the towel and snapped it expertly against her bare legs.

"Ow!"

He took off running, and she chased after him, her threats of retaliation and his laughter filling the quiet spaces in the rooms around them.

By mid-October, the Halloween Carnival committee had plans under control. "I can't believe you and Adam aren't going," Glory grumbled.

"Mickey calls," Alexis said. She was driving

her friends home from the latest planning ses-
sion. They'd stayed after school, and it was her
week to have the car. Tessa sat up front, Glory
and Charmaine in the backseat.

"Actually, I think we took the news about
being left behind very well," Charmaine said. "I
hardly even called you bad names."

"And we're proud of you," Tessa said. "Of
course, if either of you want to take my place and
baby-sit Wade—"

The two girls squealed. "No way!"

"Anybody hungry?" Alexis asked.

"Always," Tessa said.

Glory said, "I have a few bucks."

"That's a miracle," Tessa muttered.

"No fast food," Charmaine said. "I'm on a
diet."

"You're always on a diet," Glory said.

"Look . . . there's Sea Dreams." Tessa called
out the name of a popular seafood place off the
main thoroughfare. "Fish is good for us."

"Too expensive," Charmaine said.

"My treat," Alexis said, turning into the parking lot.

"Since when?" Tessa asked.

"Since no one's cooking at my house. Mom
gave me a fifty this morning." Alexis couldn't

forget how her mother had rushed into the kitchen and shoved bills into her hand and Adam's. "Got a huge fund-raiser tonight. I'll be really late, so take yourselves to dinner. See you." And then she was out the door.

"Wow," Glory said. "All my mom gave me this morning was a hard time."

They all laughed as Alexis parked. Inside, the restaurant was lit by twinkling lights and candles. "Four for nonsmoking," Alexis said. "We'd like a booth, please."

The hostess eyed them skeptically but picked up menus. "Right this way."

They followed her single file, weaving their way among crowded tables. "She probably thinks we only go out on prom night," Tessa whispered from behind Alexis.

But Alexis wasn't listening. On the other side of the room, at a table for two, she had seen her father. He was sitting with a pretty, young blond woman, and they were leaning into each other, their gazes on each other's faces, their hands touching slightly, wineglasses filled beside them. Alexis stopped so abruptly that the others plowed into her.

"Ouch," Glory said when Charmaine clipped her heel.

Alexis spun. "I've changed my mind," she said. "I don't want to eat here."

"But I do," Charmaine said. "I'm really getting into thoughts of lobster."

Tessa's gaze shifted, and Alexis felt her cheeks burn because she knew Tessa had seen her father and the woman too. Tessa grabbed Glory by the shoulders, turned her and gently edged her back toward the front door. "Come on, ladies. Let's pick some other place to eat."

"But why?" Charmaine dogged behind Glory and Tessa.

"Because the girl with the money has changed her mind about having fish," she said.

"Are you sure? I didn't hear Alexis say a word about fish."

Alexis was out the door, so she missed Tessa's comeback. Outside, she took in great gulps of evening air. Her hands shook, and she felt numb, recalling the look of rapt attention and tenderness on her father's face.

"*Hellloo . . .*"

Alexis was suddenly aware of Glory peering hard at her.

"Want to tell us what's going on?"

"I—I just changed my mind about eating

there, that's all. It smelled nasty and was giving me a headache."

"If not here, where?" Charmaine asked testily.

"Can we do it some other time?"

"Fine with me," Tessa said cheerfully, going toward the car. "Want me to drive?"

Alexis met her friend's gaze, but shook her head. "It's all right. I'll drive."

Her hands shook as she inserted the key into the ignition. She backed out of the lot with a screech and floored the accelerator to get into the flow of traffic.

"Don't kill us," Charmaine said.

Tessa blasted the radio so that no one could talk on the ride home.

SIX

Alexis told no one about seeing her father with another woman, not even Adam. Tessa said, "It was probably harmless," when she talked to her later in the week.

" 'Harmless' is being there with Mom."

They were in the library again, studying for a political science test.

"There's probably a good explanation." Tessa tried again.

"Like what? I've tried to think of good explanations. But the way he was looking at her—" Alexis's voice caught.

"I don't know, but parents are strange animals, and they do strange things."

"What if it was your father?"

"My father? The only restaurants he frequents are the ones with menus posted on the walls."

"This is serious."

"I know." Tessa sounded contrite. "If you really want to know what's going on, maybe you should ask him."

"I can't do that. Not now." How did Alexis explain to Tessa about her parents' war zone at their house? "You won't say anything, will you? I—I can trust you not to blab this around, can't I?"

"How can you ask that? Of course I won't."

"You may be right about there being a good explanation." Alexis wanted to drop the subject. It was giving her a headache, and thinking about it all the time was tying her stomach in knots. She wondered how many of her father's late nights had been spent with this woman. She shook her head and took deep breaths. She hated the direction her mind was going in and forced her thoughts to return to images of her father calmly reading the paper in the den, and organizing stacks of paint cans in the garage, and practicing his golf putt in the backyard. *That* was her father, not the man looking into the eyes of the unknown woman at a public restaurant.

A public restaurant! Of course, why hadn't she thought of that before? If something clandestine was happening, why would he choose a

restaurant as popular as Sea Dreams, where anybody could see him? She quietly shared her revelation with Tessa.

"Good thought," Tessa said, beaming Alexis a
smile. "Very good thought. You're a born debater,
Alexis. You see both sides of a situation and
think them through. If this had been an actual
debate and I was a judge, I'd give you the round."

For the first time that afternoon, Alexis
smiled. "You're prejudiced."

"True, but it's still a good argument."

Alexis pretended to return to studying, but
her thoughts wouldn't stop spinning. She had
devised a logical excuse. Now she and Tessa
could stop thinking and talking about seeing her
father with another woman. But her explanation
gave her no real peace. Which was the whole
problem with mistrust. Once it began to grow, it
was like a weed that couldn't be killed.

At the end of the month, Alexis and her friends
drove two cars to Disney World in drizzling rain,
keeping in contact via rearview mirrors and cell
phones. Sawyer led the caravan with Alexis and
Tessa in his car. Adam followed in his and
Alexis's car with Kelly and Wade. If Wade had
been disappointed with Tessa's choice to ride

without him, he hadn't let on. "No way do I want him to think of us as a couple," Tessa told Alexis before they left the driveway.

"No problem," Alexis said. She knew that riding with Adam and Kelly would have been difficult for Tessa. During the long drive Alexis played a book on tape; then Sawyer switched to his favorite CDs. They ate lunch at a fast-food place along the way.

At Disney World, they checked into two reserved suites at a hotel inside the grounds. When the three girls threw open the door to their room, Kelly said, "Wow. Pretty nice."

"Yes. Well, Dad wanted us to have the best," Alexis said. She was determined to spare no expense on the trip. It would serve her father right if she maxed out his card. They each made perfunctory calls home to say they had arrived safely, then set out with the guys to explore the Magic Kingdom.

"Where to first?" Adam asked on the monorail ride into the heart of the park.

"Space Mountain," everyone said in unison.

The line to ride the roller coaster was short because of the light rain, so they got in without much of a wait. Strapped into the seat, Alexis cuddled against Sawyer. "Okay," he said as the ride started to move, "I'll be Worf the Klingon like in *Star Trek*, and you can be Counselor Deanna Troi, that psychic woman."

"She's an empath," Alexis said. "And why her?"

He nuzzled Alexis's neck. "Because she's pretty, like you are. And because she always knows what others are thinking and feeling. And because she ended up loving big ugly Worf."

Alexis felt a melting sensation. "You're not ugly."

He laughed. "Thank you, counselor. So tell me, what else am I thinking?"

The roller coaster began to climb slowly inside Space Mountain, and twinkling lights representing planets and stars emerged.

Alexis pressed her fingers against her temples. "I'm seeing a soccer trophy in the spring."

"True. But it's not spring yet. What am I thinking right now?" He leaned closer.

"That you're going to—" She got no further, because the coaster made it over the first hill and went hurtling down into the dark. Her stomach fell, and she grabbed hold of Sawyer's arm. "Hang on!"

"You hang on!" Sawyer shouted above the roar of the machine. "To me!"

From the seat behind them, she heard Kelly shriek. Alexis watched the stars fly past as the coaster whipped around the galaxy, barely missing an asteroid heading toward them. She ducked reflexively and felt Sawyer's arm tighten around her. "Scared?" he shouted.

"No way!"

The ride through outer space took only a few minutes, yet left Alexis breathless and exhilarated. When the coaster rolled to a stop at the space station, she turned toward Adam. "Let's do it again."

"Sounds good to me."

"Not me," Kelly said. She looked woozy.

Adam caught her around the waist. "Maybe you'd better sit for a minute." He led her to a bench. The light, misty rain had stopped, and the sun was attempting to make an appearance.

"You didn't think that was fun?" Alexis asked.

"I hardly ever have fun while nauseous."

Tessa and Wade came up to them. "That was a blast," Tessa said. "Who's up for another go?"

"Kelly's a little shaky," Alexis said.

Kelly looked at the others. "You all go on. I'll wait here for you."

"I won't leave you," Adam said, sitting beside her.

Kelly said, "No, really. Go. Roller coasters just aren't for me."

"How about the merry-go-round?" Wade asked, his tone condescending.

"Knock it off," Adam said. "She can't help it if she doesn't like coasters."

"I've got it," Sawyer interjected. "We'll flip a coin to see who sits it out with Kelly. That's how we decide things on our soccer team."

"Seems fair," Alexis said. She could tell Adam really wanted to go again, and she didn't want him to miss out.

"That's okay with me," Kelly said.

Sawyer took out a quarter and paired off with Alexis. "Call it."

"Heads."

"Heads it is. I lost that round. Alexis is riding. I'll flip with Adam."

"Tails," Adam said.

"You win." Sawyer lost to Tessa too, so only he and Wade were left. Alexis had her fingers crossed that Wade would lose the call, because if he did, Tessa would ride with Adam and she with Sawyer, while Wade baby-sat Kelly. Perfect.

Wade lost the toss, and Alexis could barely suppress her smile. Looking dejected, Wade sat.

Tessa said, "Tell you what. After this ride, I'll go with you again."

Kelly smiled weakly. "I'm really sorry I have such a touchy stomach."

"Not a problem," Alexis said.

"Take it easy," Adam said. "We'll be back soon. Wade, you take care of my girl."

Wade saluted.

Alexis knew she didn't dare look Tessa in the eye for fear of making them both giggle uncontrollably. She and Sawyer fell into step behind Adam and Tessa, heading for the short line at the start of the ride.

Sawyer took her hand. "Why do you look so happy? Did I miss something?"

"Not a thing."

"But you are happy about something, aren't you?"

"I'm happy because I'm with you, Mr. Worf."

Adam turned. "Mr. Worf?"

"Inside joke," Alexis said.

Sawyer shrugged. "She's clairvoyant," he said to Adam. "Didn't you know?"

"You're both nuts," Adam said with a grin.

"Let's go, Number One," Tessa said, catching on to the *Star Trek* lingo immediately.

"Well, if I'm Number One, who are you—the captain?" Adam asked.

"Oh no. . . . We can't all be officers. Just think of me as just another dreamer aboard the starship."

Adam grinned. Sawyer tightened his hold on Alexis's hand. And Alexis silently wished that Kelly wouldn't be waiting when the ride was over.

SEVEN

But Kelly *was* waiting, and she looked a whole lot perkier. Adam put his arm around her, and Tessa fell back alongside Wade. They toured the area, and dusk was falling when Sawyer announced, "I'm hungry."

"You're always hungry," Alexis said.

"I'm a growing boy."

"Let's go to the Hard Rock Cafe," Wade said. "I know there's one on the grounds."

"Hotel first," Adam said. "I want to grab something from the room."

Alexis thought Adam's request was odd, but Kelly thought it was a good idea because she wanted to get her sweater.

The group caught the monorail back to the hotel and were met in the lobby by a pretty girl dressed as a hula dancer. "It's luau night," she told them as she draped colorful leis around their necks. "Big party by the indoor pool. Live rock band and free food. No crowds either. Come join us."

"Rock band?" Sawyer's face lit up. "We can do Hard Rock tomorrow night."

"Get your bathing suits," the dancer urged. "The pool's heated."

In the elevator, Tessa groused, "I *hate* bathing suits. Mine is so old."

Of course, Alexis knew that Tessa felt self-conscious in a bathing suit and had only brought one because Alexis had insisted. "It'll be fine," she said.

"You can borrow one of mine. I brought two." Kelly's big blue eyes looked innocent as she made her offer.

When Kelly stepped into the bathroom to change, Tessa said, "Was she being hateful? She must know I couldn't squeeze into one of hers even if I greased myself all over with olive oil."

Alexis said, "Ignore her. I'm not sure that her mouth and her brain are in constant communication."

Tessa giggled. "Well, I did get to ride Space Mountain with Adam. And I sat as close to him as I dared. Maybe she's miffed about it."

"Who cares? Just forget about her and have a good time."

"It isn't easy seeing her with him, you know. Not that I have one chance in a million with him myself."

"Are you sorry you came?"

Tessa thought about the question before saying, "No. Just being around him is a high for me. Even if Kelly is permanently attached to his side."

Alexis thought instantly of seeing her father in the restaurant with the pretty younger woman instead of her mother. "Nothing's permanent," she said.

Down at the pool, a small band dressed in surfer shorts and Hawaiian shirts played for about sixty people. Buffet tables were laden with hot and cold hors d'oeuvres, platters of fresh vegetables and sliced fruit and trays heaped with bite-sized desserts. Wade and Sawyer were already in the water, but Adam sat in a lounge chair wearing long black spandex bicycle pants and a shirt.

"What's with the outfit?" Alexis asked, dropping her towel onto his chair.

"When I was packing, I grabbed the wrong thing out of my drawer."

"Does that mean you won't come swimming?" Kelly sounded disappointed.

"I'm swimming—if you don't mind being with someone who looks this nerdy."

Sawyer came out of the pool when he saw Alexis. "I told him to just wear a pair of shorts."

Adam shrugged. "I didn't bring any spares."

Alexis said, "Well, you do look nerdy."

"So sue me." He took Kelly's hands. "You look great. Go on in. I'll save us a table, then jump in." He urged her toward the water, then began gathering chairs around a poolside table, staking a claim with extra towels draped over the chair backs.

Sawyer grabbed Alexis's hand. "Let's go down the water slide."

"I thought you were starving."

"I am, but we may as well wait until the line goes down."

She looked over to see guests clustered around the buffet. The band began a loud tune, and the next thing Alexis knew, she was climbing the ladder for the slippery glide down into the heated aqua water of the pool. Soon Tessa, Wade, Adam and Kelly were sliding with them, one right after another, reminding Alexis of playful seals. She lost count of the number of times she climbed the ladder. At some point they stopped long enough to sit and eat at the table Adam had saved.

They were finishing up when Kelly pointed and said, "Look."

Underwater lights were turning the pool's water shades of yellow, green, blue, red and orange in rhythm to the music from the band, just back from a break. From the sides of the pool, water shot from almost invisible hoses. The streams met in the air before falling in cascades of lighted rainbows onto the surface. As lights shimmered and the water danced, the audience broke out in applause.

When the water show was over, a volleyball net was stretched across the water and an invitation was issued for the guests to choose up sides. "All right," Sawyer said with a grin, and rubbed his hands together. "Come on, guys. We can take on anybody."

Alexis felt her own competitive spirit rise.

Kelly stood and started for the water. Adam didn't follow, so she asked, "You coming?"

"I think I'll sit out for a while. You go on and play."

Kelly glanced longingly at the water. "I should stay with you."

"Why? Truth is, I'm not very good at volley-ball."

His excuse surprised Alexis because he was good at the land version of the game. "You doing all right?" she asked.

"Doing great. I just don't want to play. I'll kick back and watch you guys destroy all comers. That okay with you, *Mother?*"

The others laughed at Alexis's expense. "Gee, excuse me for asking a question," Alexis said.

"And excuse me for taking a break. What are you, my parole officer? Jeez, Ally, butt out."

His words stung. "Didn't know you could be so touchy."

"Didn't know you could be so nosy." Adam looked at Sawyer. "Does she nag you like she does me?"

Alexis felt color creep into her cheeks.

"Love is blind," Sawyer said good-naturedly.

"But not silent," Adam said.

"Now, children, let's behave," Tessa said.

A whistle blew, and Sawyer took Alexis's arm. "Save it for the match, tiger."

Privately, Alexis seethed as she went into the water. Adam had no right to bite her head off and embarrass her in front of the others. All she'd done was ask if he was all right, and he'd picked a fight with her. *Not fair!*

"Heads up!" Sawyer called, and Alexis snapped out of her funk in time to see the ball headed straight for her. She smacked it hard, and within minutes she had forgotten about her tiff with Adam.

Their little team kept winning because Tessa turned out to have a fantastic serve and Kelly a mean spike.

"Way to go, Kelly," Wade said after she had almost stuffed the ball down a guy's throat on the other side of the net.

"I like to pretend the ball's my math teacher's head," she said with a blue-eyed innocence that made the others laugh.

The opposition dwindled until theirs was the only team remaining. Finally, they were declared the official champions of the event, and as they climbed out of the water to get their individual plastic trophies, Alexis looked over at the table where Adam had been sitting. His chair was empty.

Later, in the room, Kelly asked, "Do you think he left because he's mad at us?"

"Why should he be mad at us? He had his chance to play," Alexis said, irritated with her brother all over again. They were getting ready for bed, and Tessa was in the bathroom brushing her teeth.

"Maybe I should call him," Kelly said. She kept fidgeting with her hair and looking insecure.

"Feel free."

Kelly grabbed the receiver and punched in Adam's room number. Alexis tried not to listen while Kelly talked, but when it seemed as if they were about to hang up, she asked Kelly for the phone. "It's me, your nosy sister," she said. "You know, the one with the genuine gold plastic trophy for winning at water volleyball."

He chuckled. "And this is me, your sorry brother. I shouldn't have gotten hot with you. Are we straight now?"

She shrugged, feeling her irritation melting. "I guess so. I didn't mean to go off on you. I just didn't understand why you wouldn't play."

"I thought you all were a better team without me. Besides, it gave you girls a chance to show your stuff."

His explanation made sense. With him on the

team, someone else would have had to sit out. Probably Tessa. "Where did you go, anyway?"

"I played video games with some kid named Marshall. He was stuck in a wheelchair, Ally. I felt bad for him because no one was paying him any mind, and I know what that feels like."

She understood instantly. Adam's long periods of isolation in the hospital had given him a heightened sense of compassion for others, especially for those who didn't quite fit into the mainstream. "I hate it when you pull out that kindness card," she said, feeling contrite. "It makes the rest of us seem so shallow."

"Just putting myself in others' shoes. The guy seemed lonely. I know how that feels. So we went inside and spent some time on the video machines. He trounced me too."

"Well, maybe he'll give you a rematch. We still have all day tomorrow and half of Sunday before we have to return to the real world."

"True. Sawyer wants to tell you good night, so don't hang up. You and Tessa take good care of my girl, you hear?"

Alexis glanced over at Kelly, curled up on the sleeper sofa reading a teen magazine. Her sleek blond hair caught the lamp's light, and with her face scrubbed clean, she looked about twelve. "Will do," Alexis said with a sigh, wishing with all her might that she liked the girl as much as Adam did. "Put Sawyer on."

"Hey, babe," he said when he came on the line. "Dream of me, okay?"

"And you dream of me," she answered.

"I always do, baby. I always do."

EIGHT

On Saturday, the group met for an early breakfast in the hotel dining room. The rain clouds were gone, and sunlight streamed through spotless windows looking out onto gardens of colorful hibiscus, roses and creamy white gardenias. Tessa, last through the buffet line, sat down in the booth with a groan.

"What's wrong with you?" Wade asked.

"Every muscle in my body aches. Who knew a game played in water could hurt so much the next day?"

"I'm sore too," Alexis said, rotating her shoulders. "I'm sticking with the debate team from now on."

"I feel fine," Kelly said, sipping orange juice and looking bouncy.

Between mouthfuls of scrambled eggs, Sawyer

said, "Take a hot shower and hit the weight room. That'll work out the kinks."

Tessa gave him a sour look. "I'm talking major knots here, Sawyer."

"Try a massage."

"I could give you a rubdown," Wade offered.

"Down, boy," Adam said.

"What? My aunt's a massage therapist."

"Good one," Sawyer said.

"No . . . really. She is." He flexed his fingers.

"Let your fingers do the walking," Adam said. He and Sawyer exchanged high fives across the table.

"Keep your fingers away from my body, buster," Tessa growled.

"You've been warned," Alexis said, smiling.

"Why are you all picking on Wade?" Kelly asked, bewildered. "He's just trying to be helpful."

Adam said, "You're right. We should cut him some slack."

"Why?" Sawyer wanted to know. "Wade's cool about it, aren't you, Wade?"

"Doesn't bother me," Wade said.

"But it's bothering Kelly," Adam said.

Alexis rolled her eyes, and Adam warned away any of her comments with a look. "Okay," she said, suddenly all business. "Let's plan our agenda for the day." She pulled out a map of the Magic Kingdom and spread it out over the breakfast plates. In no time, she had prepared a list that included everybody's choices.

"What if we finish and have time left over?" Adam asked.

"Disney isn't the only attraction in Orlando," Alexis said. "We have cars. We can get to others."

They were in agreement, but when they all stood to leave, Adam took his sister's elbow and pulled her aside. "Other attractions? You're really sticking it to Dad, aren't you?"

"He could have brought us and controlled spending."

Adam's eyes narrowed. "Is there something you're not telling me?"

She didn't meet his gaze, because the image of her father with the other woman jumped into her mind, and although she knew it was impossible, she was concerned that Adam might see it in her eyes. "Nothing," she said. "Come on. Let's go have some fun."

They spent the day hitting every ride in the park, including the ones targeted at small children.

Kelly refused to consider another roller coaster, and even got queasy riding the teacups. She insisted that Adam ride the coasters without her, but he stayed with her while the others rode, which irked Alexis. She didn't think it was fair that he should have to skip what she knew were his favorite rides because of Kelly. "She's my girl," he said to Alexis when she told him as much out of earshot of the others. "I like being with her, even if it means not riding anything at all. She can't help it if some of the rides make her sick."

Alexis wasn't sure, but she kept her opinion to herself.

When they came to It's a Small World, Adam balked.

"Come on," Alexis urged. "It'll be like when we were little."

"I don't think so, Ally. You made us go on it six times when we were little. I've never recovered."

Alexis turned to Sawyer, who backed away. "I don't mind sitting this one out myself, babe."

"Party poopers," Alexis said with a toss of her head. "Anyone coming with me?"

There were no takers, so she climbed aboard and went by herself. The ride was boring, but she enjoyed the sense of nostalgia she experienced. As she had during the time capsule ceremony weeks before, Alexis recalled simpler days, before Adam got sick and before her parents were constantly at odds. She closed her eyes, conjured up the photograph of her family from the bulletin board in her room. In a moment of remorse, she'd dug it out of the trash and taped the pieces back together. Yet try as she might, she couldn't hold on to the image; reality nudged it aside. The happy smiles dissolved into angry scowls. Adam morphed from a soft-cheeked child into a gaunt preteen, bald from chemo treatments. Her own expression went from delighted to fearful.

She opened her eyes and stared hard at the scenery surrounding her. The puppets looked tired and trite, and the music began to grate on her nerves. It had been a mistake to go on the ride. She wasn't nine anymore. The magic was gone.

Sawyer was there to meet her when the ride ended, and she fairly jumped out of the seat and into his arms when the carts stopped. "Wow— this is cool. Did you miss me that much?" he asked, a silly grin on his face.

"Longest ten minutes of the day. Where are the others?"

"Everybody went off in different directions. We're supposed to meet up at six by the lake. We're on our own."

She shook off the last vestiges of her disappointment with the ride and asked, "So where do you want to go?"

"Anywhere that I can kiss you a hundred times uninterrupted."

She shoved him playfully. "Second choice?"

"The closest coaster."

They took off hand in hand and rode every daredevil coaster in the park for the second time that day.

Alexis couldn't sleep. After watching the Disney parade on Main Street and the fireworks over Cinderella's castle, she and her friends had played the video machines in the hotel game room. Around two A.M. they told one another good night and went to their rooms, insisting that they would all sleep in. They didn't have to check out until noon, and it was a long drive back to Miami. Tessa and Kelly were sleeping soundly and Alexis didn't want to disturb them, but she also hated lying in the dark wide awake. Finally, around five, she got up, dressed quietly and took the elevator down to the indoor pool.

She told herself she'd watch the sun come up, then go back to bed and grab some sleep.

Outside the floor-to-ceiling windows, it was still pitch-dark. Underwater lights made the patio area glow eerily. She was heading toward a lounge chair when she realized she wasn't alone. She stopped short, surprised that anyone else was up so early. The person, half hidden by the back of a lounger, turned. She was looking at Adam.

"What are you doing here?" she asked.

"Couldn't sleep. And you?"

"Same problem." She took the chair beside his. "Maybe our twin radar is working overtime."

Adam said, "Sawyer snores like a buzz saw. Do you know that?"

Color crept up her cheeks. "How would I know something like that?"

He grinned but didn't comment.

"As long as we're swapping intimate information, Kelly talks in her sleep," Alexis said coolly.

"I'd love to hear her sometime."

"She mumbles. . . . Can't understand a word."

Adam looked out over the water, his expression pensive. "You still ticked at Dad for not making this a family vacation?"

"Not just Dad. Mom too. They acted like a family vacation was a death sentence."

"Be honest—isn't it a whole lot more fun being here with our friends than with our parents?"

Naturally he was right. Being stuck with their parents for three days might not have been much fun at all. "I guess it was just the way they handled it. If for one minute they had even *acted* like they'd wanted to come, to be with us and with each other, then I'd feel better about it. You know what our house feels like?"

"You mean besides tense?"

She swung her body around so that she was facing her brother. "It feels like a marina. Boats pull in and dock. They pull out to go off on the water alone. Their hulls don't touch. Their berths don't switch. Dock and go." She motioned with her hand. "Little ships without contact."

"Come September, we can set our own course."

"And don't think I'm not looking forward to it. I'm not sure what I'll do if I don't get accepted to Stetson."

"You'll pick another college."

She wrinkled her nose. "I don't want another college. Would you want to switch from baseball to soccer?"

"It's too late for me."

"Maybe too late to retrain your feet, but not your hands. You could be a goalie, like Sawyer."

Adam shook his head. "No way."

Through the windows, dawn streaked the sky with color. Alexis watched darkness fade to gray, then lighten to soft pink. "It's going to be a beautiful day. Too bad we have to leave paradise."

"Yes, too bad," Adam said, his gaze on the brightening sky.

"You tired?" she asked.

"Not a bit."

"The breakfast buffet opens at six," she said, scooting off the lounger. "And all of a sudden, I'm starved. Let's go raid it."

"What about the others?"

"We can eat again with them."

He grinned. "Eat breakfast twice? You up for that?"

"Absolutely." She reached out and squeezed his upper arm through his jacket. "Besides, I think you're looking a little skinny these days. Look how your jacket's hanging on you."

"Part of my plan," he said smoothly. "Bulk up with muscle, not fat. It's hard for a butterball to move very fast on the playing field, you know."

They headed inside to the buffet table.

The ride home was subdued. "Do we have to go back?" Wade asked before piling into Adam's car.

"Sorry, the party's over," Alexis told him. She was already thinking about undone assignments and incomplete homework. She and Tessa had a county-wide debate coming up in mid-November, and she'd barely started on her position paper for it. Then there was an English paper, and tests to face in four of her six courses—all before the Thanksgiving holiday.

They didn't arrive in the city until after eight. Sawyer dropped off Tessa, while Adam took Wade and then Kelly home. They met up in a fast-food parking lot near the school at Alexis's insistence. "I can take you home," Sawyer said, sounding unhappy with her plan to ride home with her brother and not him.

"I'll go with Adam. We're already much later than we said we'd be."

Sawyer kissed her lightly before she scooted into the car. "I'll see you tomorrow, then."

"Tomorrow." She waved as Adam backed the car out.

"I had a good time," Adam said as he drove toward their house.

"Me too."

"Thanks for coming up with the idea and getting Mom and Dad to agree. And thanks for being nice to Kelly too. I know you're not crazy about her."

She started to protest but knew it would be hypocritical. "She's lucky you like her. Think of all the girls who are eating their hearts out because you picked her instead of them." Of course, Alexis was thinking of Tessa.

"You're a riot," Adam said, raising the garage door with the touch of a button. "Truth is, nobody wanted me when I was on chemo. Nobody."

"That's all over now," she said sympathetically. "You're healthy, wealthy and wise."

He popped the trunk with the lever under his seat. "Not wealthy after this weekend. When are you going to give those receipts to Dad?"

She giggled and hopped out of the car. "When Visa sends him a bill, of course. No use risking being grounded before then."

NINE

"Are you sure you don't want to come down to campaign headquarters and watch the election results come in with me?" Eleanor poked her head into Alexis's room as she spoke. "You'll get to see the American system at work firsthand. Maybe pick up extra points for that poli sci class of yours."

"I can't vote, Mom, and no, hanging around Pressman headquarters isn't my idea of a good time." Alexis never looked up from her computer screen.

"He's going to win, you know." Her mother sounded defensive.

Just then, Alexis's father passed by the doorway. "Good," he said. "Then maybe you can move back home."

Eleanor whirled. "I don't need your sarcasm,

Blake. I've worked hard for this victory, and it's going to help me a great deal once he's in office. And if you'd think about it instead of griping about it, it could help you too."

Blake waved her off. "I'm going to the club."

Alexis took a bite from a peanut-butter sandwich on a plate beside her keyboard. *Supper*. "I've got homework," she said.

"Where's Adam?"

"At Kelly's."

Her mother stood at the doorway, as if reluctant to leave. "Most of the results will be in by eleven. There'll be a victory party."

"So you'll be in late." Alexis finished the logical progression of her mother's sentences.

"I don't like your tone, young lady. And I sure as heck don't owe you an apology for what I do with my time."

Alexis threw up her hands, rotated her desk chair to face the doorway. "Didn't mean to rain on your parade. Go. Toast Larry Pressman's victory. See you tomorrow."

Anger flashed across her mother's face. Alexis held her breath, knowing she'd pushed pretty hard. "I need a life too," Eleanor said. "Or is that forbidden?"

"You have a life, Mother. In fact, sometimes it

seems like you have so much of a life that the rest of us are in your way."

Her mother darted into the room, eyes blazing, and for a minute Alexis thought she might get slapped. Eleanor stopped short, glaring at Alexis. "I'm not going to let you spoil this evening for me, Ally. But you had better watch your mouth. You have no idea what my life is like. What it's been like these past years. You have no idea at all."

Alexis sat very still, knowing that the least provocation might send her mother over the edge. Her heart thumped hard as the standoff lengthened. Finally, her mother turned and stalked out of the room. Minutes later, Alexis heard the front door slam. She went cold all over, struggling to understand the terrible anger inside her mother and the sense of abandonment she felt from her father. What was happening to them? Why was it happening? Was it something lacking in her and Adam? Alexis tried so hard to be a good student, to excel. How had she let them down?

The phone rang, and she jumped. Grabbing the receiver, she said, "Hello?"

"Hey, babe."

"Sawyer." She sniffed, realizing that her cheeks were wet.

"You crying?"

She wiped her eyes. "No. I think I'm getting the sniffles."

"I'm not scared of catching it. Can I come over?"

"I've got a paper due—"

"Who doesn't? Look, I'll bring some popcorn and soda and we can watch that TV show you like on Tuesday nights."

Trust Sawyer to remember her favorite TV shows. She softened. "They'll probably break in with election coverage."

"We can ignore it."

She knew he was waiting for her answer. Well, why not? She wouldn't be able to study any more that night, anyway. "Come on over," she said.

"On my way." She heard his grin through the phone line.

At eleven o'clock that night, with two-thirds of the precincts reporting, Larry Pressman was declared the city-wide winner. Alexis sat curled on sofa with Sawyer draped across her lap and

watched as the channel four news team showed
the victory celebration at the Hilton ballroom.
Pressman stood at a podium with his wife and
three kids, waving at the cameras and his jubi-
lant supporters. Balloons and streamers fell from
the ceiling. Alexis saw her mother standing off to
one side, clapping and smiling. "Hey, there's your
mom!" Sawyer said, tossing a piece of popcorn at
the screen. It bounced off Eleanor's electronic
image.

"That's her." Alexis aimed the remote and
flipped the channel.

"Don't you want to watch?"

"Why? I know she's happy. She's worked for
months for this."

"*You* don't sound too happy about it."

"Who cares? It's what she wants."

Sawyer swung his legs to the floor and scooted
upright. "What's going on, babe?"

"My family's falling apart." She hadn't meant
to tell him that, but the words had rushed out in
a wave of unshed tears.

"Hey, come on. It's okay." His arms went
around her, and she sank against his chest.

She cried a little before saying, "I just don't
know what's happening to us, Sawyer. It's like my

parents hate each other. And maybe me and Adam too."

"You know that's not true. Didn't they just let you have a blowout at Disney World? That's not because they hate you."

She pulled away as another thought hit her. "What if they get a divorce?"

"That wouldn't be your fault."

"But what if they do?"

"Half the kids in our school have divorced parents. And remarried parents."

"You don't."

He shrugged. "They fight."

"How do people fall out of love? It's not supposed to be that way."

He searched her face. "Maybe they don't. Maybe they just lose their way."

She told him then about seeing her father in the restaurant. He could say nothing to console her about that. He leaned his forehead in to touch hers. "These are supposed to be the best years of our lives."

"You're joking, right?"

"Just quoting my grandma, who says she knows these things."

She managed a laugh. "I'm glad you

came over tonight. I really didn't want to be alone."

"Me too." He lifted her chin and, with great tenderness, kissed her mouth.

Alexis threw herself into schoolwork, especially preparation for the upcoming debate. The topic for the tournament, *Resolved: That the federal government should establish an education policy to significantly increase academic achievement in secondary schools*, wasn't overly intriguing to her, but she prepared her affirmative arguments thoroughly. The burden of proof always lay with the affirmative position, and winning the round meant swaying the judges to accept her position and award her team points.

Cory, a junior, would be responsible for presenting the case and plan. Tessa would offer rebuttal when the opposition presented the negative side of the position. Following cross-examination periods between the speeches, it would fall to Alexis to summarize and cover all affirmative positions and negative rebuttals. This place on the team was usually reserved for the best speaker because it was the most difficult.

The day of the tournament, Alexis felt pumped up and ready. While Mrs. Wiley signed in the team at the site of the debate, Tessa whispered to Alexis, "You're top dog, girlfriend."

"What do you mean?" Alexis pinned her name tag to her blazer. Mrs. Wiley insisted that the team wear navy blazers and white oxford shirts when they competed.

"Everybody's looking at you."

Alexis glanced around, and sure enough, teams from other schools were giving her the once-over. Most turned away when she caught their eyes. "Wonder why. Is something wrong with me?"

"R-E-S-P-E-C-T," Tessa spelled. "Your reputation has them scared. You're a legend."

"And you're hallucinating. They're just sizing up the competition."

"No. . . . It's you they fear."

"Puh-leeze," Alexis said skeptically. "It's our whole team."

Tessa smiled. "Well, bring 'em on. I feel lucky today."

"You nut." Alexis shook her friend's shoulder.

Holding a packet, Mrs. Wiley walked up to her students. "I have our schedule. Shall we proceed to round one?"

Alexis fell into step behind their teacher and coach, with the other team members behind her.

She walked quickly through the lobby area and toward the verbal battle she hoped would take her one step closer to the state finals and admission to Stetson. She hoped her parents would hold it together until after she and Adam were out the door.

"Chalk up another one." Sawyer made an imaginary mark in the air above Alexis.

"Oh now, winning isn't everything," Alexis said with a satisfied smile.

Tessa, wearing a bigger smile, leaned into Alexis. "It's the *only* thing," they said in unison, then burst out laughing. They were standing in the hall the next day after school, waiting for Adam so that they could ride home together.

"How should we celebrate?" Sawyer asked.

"Ice cream usually works for me," Alexis said.

Charmaine and Glory butted into the group. Glory said, "Heard you brought home a trophy."

"We survived," Alexis said. She felt exhilarated. Their team had taken first place and had placed in the top three in the individual events of every category they had entered. Her original oratory had taken first place.

"The queen rules," Tessa said with a curtsy toward Alexis.

"Cut it out."

Adam walked up with Kelly. "Do I have to bow to you too?"

She checked him over. He was grinning, but he looked pale to her. "Off with his head," Alexis said, snapping her fingers.

Kelly ducked under Adam's arm and hugged him protectively. "I like his head."

"All right, all right . . . who's up for ice cream?" Sawyer called out.

The entire group stormed the door.

At the ice cream parlor, they commandeered two tables and ordered a special called the kitchen sink, which consisted of a scoop of each of the parlor's twenty-one flavors, ten toppings, butterscotch and hot fudge sauces and a can of whipped cream. It was served in a washtub, with spoons for everyone. Sawyer had insisted that the waiters and waitresses sing and clap for Alexis and Tessa as if it were their birthday. "We're celebrating," he said. "And we want to be entertained."

Much later, when they had all gone their separate ways, Alexis sat alone with Sawyer in his car at the mall. "That was fun," she told him. "Thanks for making such a big deal out of a little debate win."

"You're doing better than the football team," he reminded her.

"That's true," she said with a laugh.

"Besides, I like seeing you happy."

She closed her eyes and snuggled against him. "I think my sugar high's wearing off."

"Want a burger?"

"No . . . I'm really stuffed." Suddenly she bolted upright as a sensation of dread shot through her like an electric current. Her heart raced, and she could hardly catch her breath.

"What's the matter?" Sawyer's eyes were wide with alarm. "You look like you've seen a ghost."

"Take me home," she managed to say.

"But why—"

She grabbed his arm. "Something terrible has happened to Adam."

"How do you know?"

Fear surged through her. "I just know, all right? Hurry!"

TEN

Sawyer shoved the car into gear and took off. Alexis sat tight-lipped, fear ripping through her like waves slamming the shore. She could not quash the sense of foreboding. Something was wrong with her brother. In her driveway, she jumped from the car before it had rolled to a complete stop and ran for the back door.

"Wait up!" Sawyer shouted.

She tried the door, but it was locked. She fumbled in her purse for the key.

Sawyer caught up with her. "I don't think anyone's here. The garage is empty."

Where were her parents? Where was Adam? She jammed the key into the lock, opened the door and rushed inside. The kitchen was empty, all the counters clear and clean, like a galley in a spotless ship.

"Alexis . . . slow down," Sawyer was saying.

She saw a note posted on the refrigerator. In bold black writing, her mother had scrawled: *Ally—Come to Kendall Hospital ER.* Alexis jerked the paper off the fridge and handed it to Sawyer.

His eyes widened as he read it. He said, "Come on. I'll drive you."

The small emergency room of their community hospital was not crowded. The first person Alexis recognized was Kelly, sitting in a chair, clutching a jacket, her face red from crying. Alexis rushed over. "What happened?"

"Oh, Alexis . . . it was so terrible." Kelly's eyes were swollen slits, her baby-fine blond hair a tangled mess. "H-he collapsed. Just collapsed right in front of me."

Alexis knees went weak and she sank into a chair. Sawyer crouched in front of Kelly.

"Tell me exactly what happened," Alexis said.

"W-we were at my house. I kept asking him if he felt okay because he wasn't looking too good to me. He kept saying he was fine, but then suddenly he grabbed hold of the arm of the sofa and just fell down. I started screaming. My dad came running and we couldn't wake Adam up. He just lay there. Daddy called the paramedics."

Alexis felt sick to her stomach. "And my mom—?"

"Daddy called her as soon as the paramedics came. She was at home, which was lucky because Adam says she's hardly ever at home anymore. But she came straight to the hospital."

"Where is she now?"

Kelly gestured toward the doors that led to the triage area of the ER.

"Has our dad been called?"

Kelly shrugged and cried fresh tears. "Th-the paramedics asked me if Adam was high—you know, on drugs. I told them I didn't think so. That we'd just eaten ice cream . . ." She looked at Alexis. "He doesn't do drugs, does he?"

"Never." It disgusted Alexis that Kelly had even asked. She saw an admittance clerk and hurried over to the desk. "Excuse me, my brother was brought in—"

The woman interrupted her. "I haven't heard anything yet. Go sit down. I'm sure someone will talk to you soon."

"But I want to go be with him."

"I'm sorry, that's impossible."

Alexis felt like diving across the desk and grabbing the woman by the throat.

Sawyer appeared by her side, took her elbow. "Maybe you should try and call your dad's cell phone."

Of course. She tore through her purse until she found her cell, but her fingers were shaking so badly that she couldn't press the numbers on the tiny keypad.

"Here, let me." Sawyer took the phone. She gave him the number; he entered it and handed the phone back to her.

An automated voice told her that the cell user she was trying to reach wasn't available and that she should call back later. She started to heave the phone across the room, but Sawyer slid it from her hand. "Where is he?" she said fiercely under her breath. She needed her daddy and he wasn't there.

The doors of the triage area opened and her mother emerged. Alexis ran to her. "Thank God you're here," her mother said. Her face was a mask of anguish.

"Adam—" Alexis choked out.

Her mother stood stiffly and looked brittle, as if she'd break if she were even touched. "The ambulance is taking him to Jackson." She named the enormous state-of-the-art hospital in the heart of Miami. The hospital where Adam had spent so many months struggling to recover from chemo and other cancer treatments. "He's relapsed," Eleanor said in a hoarse whisper. "He's in serious trouble."

When Adam had been eleven, Alexis hadn't been allowed on the floor where he was roomed. When he'd been thirteen, she'd only been allowed to visit him in the common areas where other patients met with their families. But now she was seventeen, and she swore that no one would keep her off the oncology floor. She'd ridden to Jackson Memorial with her mother, following the ambulance, driving in a nonemergency transport mode. Sawyer was behind them in his car.

"How is he?" Alexis asked during the interminable ride.

"Very sick."

"What are they going to do for him?"

"His cancer specialist, Dr. Bernstein, will meet us at Jackson. He'll decide what to do."

In the flash of streetlights, Alexis could see that her mother was gripping the steering wheel so tightly that her knuckles looked stark white. "We were at the mall eating ice cream. He seemed fine," Alexis protested.

"He wasn't fine. And this didn't happen overnight. When they took off his shirt and pants in the ER, there were bruises all over him."

Alexis caught her breath. "How—?"

"You're probably too young to remember, but that was his first symptom when he was eleven . . . bruising for no reason."

She didn't remember, but then no one had gone out of their way to tell her either. She only remembered him getting sick and sleeping a lot.

"Back then, they thought it was a bad case of the flu, or mono, but more tests revealed that it was a whole lot worse."

"I—I thought he was better. That he was in remission and that the worst was over."

"No. It isn't." Her mother's voice cracked.

Alexis fought the urge to gag. They rode in silence with no noise but the car's heater humming on low. After a while, she said, "I tried to call Dad, but I couldn't reach him."

"He's at his office. They turn the switchboard off at night, and he didn't see fit to keep his cell phone on." Her voice had an edge to it.

"He should know."

Eleanor took a deep breath, her gaze fixed fully on the road. "He'll come home eventually. Did you leave the note?"

"I—I don't remember."

By then they were pulling into the ambulance bay. Her mother parked, and they followed the stretcher into the ER. Alexis couldn't take her eyes off her brother. He was covered with a blanket, except for one arm, which was connected to a portable IV line clamped to the stretcher. A series of ugly bruises stained his bare skin. His eyes were closed, but she saw dark circles beneath them, and his face looked downright gaunt. Why hadn't she seen this until now? They lived in the same house. She should have noticed these things.

Adam was transferred to a gurney and rolled onto an elevator. Alexis, her mother and an orderly stood silent during the trip to the oncology floor. There a nurse met them and took them to the intensive care unit. "Just until we stabilize him," the nurse explained. "Dr. Bernstein will be here shortly."

The ICU was laid out like a wheel, with the nurses' station and monitoring units at the hub and glass-fronted rooms radiating out like spokes. Alexis saw patients in some of the other rooms.

Alexis grew aware of a ruckus at the outside door of the ICU and recognized Sawyer's voice. She made it to the door in time to see a nurse barring his way. "You can't go in there," the nurse was saying. "Only immediate family."

Alexis quickly stepped into the hall. "It's all right. He's with me."

"Well, explain the rules to him," the nurse instructed. "Or I'll have to call security."

She disappeared inside the unit, and Alexis went into Sawyer's arms. He said, "I told her we were brothers."

"And she didn't believe you?"

Sawyer shrugged. "She was making me mad." He held Alexis tightly. "How's Adam?"

"Pretty sick. We're waiting for his doctor."

"Do they know what's wrong?"

"What's always been wrong—cancer." The word tasted bitter in her mouth.

"But I thought—"

"So did I."

Like Tessa, Sawyer knew about Adam's illness, mostly because of his close relationship with Alexis. "I'm really sorry," he said.

She stepped away. "What happened to Kelly?"

"Her dad took her home. She was a basket case."

"So am I. I'm just better at keeping a lid on it, I guess."

"There's a waiting room down the hall, and

some sign that says ICU patients can only be visited for ten minutes every thirty minutes. Maybe we should go set up camp in there."

She looked over her shoulder at the closed door. "I should go back."

"Your mother's there. Come sit down before you keel over."

She went with him, but only to appease him. She wanted to be in the room with Adam. The lounge was small and dimly lit by lamps. The overhead lights were off, and curtains were drawn across windows. She and Sawyer were alone in the place. "What time is it?"

"I don't have my watch."

Alexis sank into a sofa. The afternoon and the celebratory trip to the ice cream parlor seemed as if they had happened a hundred years before. "You can go home, Sawyer. I know it's late."

"I called home. My parents understand. I don't want to leave you."

She lay against his shoulder. It felt good to have him near to lean on, to be with. Someone just for her. She said, "Adam has bruises all over him. I can't understand why I didn't see them."

"He kept pretty covered up. Think about Disney World and the long pants. In the room, he wore jeans to bed. Wade and I thought it was odd, but . . ." He let the sentence trail off.

Alexis went hot and cold all over as realization dawned on her. She thought back to the way Adam had quickly covered up when he got out of the pool. And to the fact that he had been wearing long-sleeved shirts to school. "He was hiding the bruises," she said. "Because he knew."

"What did he know?" Eleanor had come into the waiting room and had walked over to the sofa without Alexis even seeing her.

Startled, Alexis looked up into her mother's stricken face. "He knew he was sick again," she said. "But he didn't want us to know."

Her mother steadied herself on the wall. "How could he do that? Why?"

"I guess we'll have to ask him, won't we?" Alexis's throat felt raw and scratchy from holding everything inside.

A man appeared in the doorway. "Eleanor? Ally? Where's Adam?"

Alexis saw her father. She jumped up from the couch, crossed the room in a few steps and flung herself into his arms. "Daddy!"

His arms tightened around her, and she dissolved into a river of white-hot tears.

ELEVEN

Alexis's father held her while her mother filled him in on what had happened. "And where's the doctor?" Blake asked when she paused.

"He's evaluating Adam now."

"We couldn't reach you, Daddy," Alexis said, her tears spent.

"I'm sorry."

Receiving no other explanation left her feeling cold and hollow.

"I'm going to see Adam and talk to that doctor," her father declared.

"We'll both go," Eleanor said.

"Me too," Alexis said.

"They won't let us all in at once, Alexis," Eleanor said. "Please wait here."

Not wanting to cause a scene, Alexis backed off. Sawyer led her to a vinyl-covered couch, where he'd made a bed for her with a pillow and a blanket. "I found the stuff in that chest over there. I guess the hospital leaves it there for families."

"I can't sleep," she said.

"Then rest until your parents come back. You look ready to explode."

"I won't let them shut me out this time," she said fiercely.

She leaned back, mostly to placate Sawyer, but he was right—she felt like a simmering volcano.

It seemed to take an eternity, but finally her parents returned. She met them in the middle of the room. "What's happening?"

Her father said, "Adam's sleeping. He's getting whole blood because his white count is off the charts. Bernstein will do a full workup tomorrow. He told us to go home."

"I'm not leaving," Alexis said. "What about you and Mom?"

"We're both staying," her mom answered.

"We should try and get some sleep," her father said. "They'll come get us if there's any change."

He settled into a lounger chair, and her mother went to a couch on the other side of the room. Alexis returned to her couch and to

Sawyer, who had thrown some cushions on the floor beside it. He covered her and lay down on the cushions, then reached up, took her hand and held it until she fell asleep.

Alexis slept fitfully. At one point, Sawyer got up and went down the hall. When he returned, he whispered, "I'm going home to clean up. I'll go to school and tell people what's going on. Kelly's version will probably sound like a disaster movie."

"Tell Tessa to call my cell phone. And tell people they shouldn't come down here, because no one can see him except us. I'll go home sometime today to shower and change, but I want to talk to Adam first. I want to know exactly how this happened. And I mean *exactly*."

Alexis ate breakfast in the hospital cafeteria with her parents. No one felt like talking. Her mother nibbled on a muffin. Her dad moved scrambled eggs around on his plate with the back of his fork. He looked disheveled, with a stubble of beard on his face, his shirt and slacks rumpled. "After we talk to the doctor, I'll go home and shower," he said. "I'll go in to the office long enough to dole out my most urgent projects."

Eleanor stared into space as if she hadn't

heard him, an expression of such sadness on her face that Alexis could hardly stand it.

Blake said, "You come with me, Ally. Do you know where Adam left your car?"

"It's probably at Kelly's."

"We'll pick it up on the way home. After we talk to the doctor, the three of us are going to sit down and talk and figure out a game plan."

"My game plan is to stay with our son," Eleanor said, her voice flat, resigned.

"Not this time," Blake said.

She stared at him in disbelief.

"We'll do this as a family," he said without apology. "No martyrs this time."

Alexis saw her mother's face go blotchy, and for an instant she thought her mother might throw something at him. Her lips compressed into a firm line, and she pushed back her chair and left the cafeteria. Her father raked his hand through his hair. Alexis was left to wonder why he had said such a thing.

He stood, scooped up his tray of uneaten food and dumped it in a nearby trash container. "Come on, honey. Let's see if your brother's awake."

Upstairs, Adam was awake, the head of his bed raised, two IV lines attached to his arm. One bag held clear liquid; another, blood. A breakfast tray that had been set on his bedside table looked untouched. He gave Alexis the once-over when she came into the room. "You look rough," he said.

"You're no vision," she answered testily, but he opened his arms and she went to him. She buried her face in his neck. Pulling back, she felt moisture filling her eyes.

"Now, don't start leaking on me." He held on to her hand. "How's Kelly?"

"Freaked out. Sawyer will check on her today."

"Tell her I'm sorry."

"Why didn't you say something to us?" Their mother came to one side of his bed, their father to the other.

"Don't gang up on me," Adam said.

"Surely you realized you weren't well," Eleanor said. "Why not tell us?"

"I didn't want it to be happening all over again. So I pretended it wasn't." Adam's tone was matter-of-fact.

"Dr. Bernstein told us you missed your lab work in August." This from Blake.

"True," Adam said.

Alexis couldn't believe what he was saying.

After his last remission, Adam had gone for lab work every six months. His last scheduled visit had been right before the time capsule ceremony at their old elementary school. As a seventeen-year-old outpatient, Adam had taken responsibility for his checkup appointments for two years, and until now, Alexis had thought he'd never missed one.

"You told us everything was good with those tests. Why did you lie to us?"

He shrugged. "I was sick and tired of the testing and then of the waiting for bad news— Were my numbers holding? Were they skewing? The pressure of always wondering sucked. So I skipped the last go-round. Bad timing. By October, I knew something was wrong, and I was pretty sure I was relapsing. I didn't want to come back here until I had to." He held his father's gaze without flinching.

Eleanor looked furious. "Dr. Bernstein told us his office called and left three messages on our home machine, plus he wrote a follow-up letter explaining how important it was for you to keep regular lab appointments. We never got any of his messages, or his letter."

Adam closed his eyes, clenched his jaw. "That's because I erased the messages. And I made sure I got to the mail first every day to intercept any letters."

"How could you? And how dare you lie to us!"

He shrugged. "I'm sorry about lying, but I wanted to go to school and have a normal life. I was tired of being micromanaged. You seemed to be relieved whenever I told you I felt fine and my checkups were good. You were busy with your job and that campaign. Dad was busy with his clients. None of us wanted to go backward, so I told you what we all wanted to hear."

Alexis's heart went out to him. She understood his logic. He had wanted to be a typical healthy teenager, even if only for a few more months. What hurt and shocked her was that he'd hid it from her so well that she'd never picked up on any of it, not even with her twin radar. She'd never suspected a thing. When he was moody, she'd chalked it up to school, Kelly, anything except a relapse.

"You almost *died*," Eleanor said, her voice shaking with emotion. "Until you got transfusions, you were all but comatose."

"Mom, I've been dying for years. A few more months of medical freedom was worth it to me."

Alexis's stomach knotted. Had he really said the word *dying*?

"Now, hold on," Blake interjected. "We're going to meet with Bernstein and the oncology staff and see what they can do to help. It's been several years since you've undergone treatments. New things have come along. New drugs and protocols. You're still going to fight."

"I never said I was quitting. I just said I wanted to be and act normal for a while. I still want that. I want to play baseball in the spring. I want to graduate in June. I'll do whatever my doctors say." He looked to his sister. "Ally will kill me if I don't graduate with her, won't you?"

"With my bare hands," she said softly, ignoring the smile he offered her.

"Then go back to school and tell my friends I'll see them soon. And—and tell Kelly that—well, that I love her."

"I'll pass it on," Alexis said, all the while wondering if the girl could handle a love as brave and determined as Adam's.

When Alexis arrived home after picking up the car, Tessa was waiting for her on the doorstep. "I cut out after third period," Tessa explained. "I was going crazy trying to sit still. I couldn't concentrate." She bit her bottom lip, as if to control her emotions. "I—I want to see him."

Alexis was sympathetic. "No one can see him except the family until he's out of ICU."

"When will that be?"

"Not sure." Alexis beckoned from the now-open front door. "Come upstairs with me while I clean up and change."

"You going back to the hospital?"

"You bet."

Tessa followed Alexis up to her room, and Alexis told her all she knew.

"I can't believe he hid this from you. That means the whole time we were running around Disney World—"

"Yes," Alexis said, grabbing clean clothes from her closet. "He's been lying about his health for months."

"Will it . . . I mean, is it going to make a difference? I mean, with the way cancer grows and spreads and all."

"I don't know." Alexis headed toward the bathroom. "But I'm sure going to find out."

Alexis didn't have a chance to be alone with Adam until that evening. Their parents were taking a much-needed break when she went into the ICU and found Adam propped up in bed, staring at the ceiling. "How's it going?" she asked.

"I've been poked and jabbed like a piece of meat all day. I don't like it any better this time than I did before."

"You look better." He wasn't as pale, and the bruising had lightened.

"Whole blood makes the difference. Now we know why vampires go after it."

"I'm really sorry, Adam."

"Me too." He turned his face away from her, and his sadness felt like a weight on her heart.

"Why did you keep it a secret?"

"I told you why. I wanted to be normal."

"Yes, but—"

"I got to have a few more months of living on the outside. It was worth it to me. And before you ask, it didn't make much of a difference in the cancer. I got sicker than if I'd checked in during September, but in the long run, I'm out of remission. End of story."

"Do you know what the doctors are going to do yet?"

"New chemo. Experimental stuff. I'll have to live here while they do it, because they'll have to keep close tabs on my blood work. The only halfway positive news is that I'll go into a private room tomorrow. I really hate the ICU."

"Well, maybe friends can come visit then." She tried to sound hopeful.

"Sure, but I have to wear a mask around visitors during the days I'm taking the drugs so they don't pass around any pesky little germs. Hey, it'll be like Halloween."

"I'll bring your schoolwork," she said.

He grimaced. "The hospital's already told me I can do homework on computers in the common room down the hall. And there's an internal channel from the school system for class lectures too. Whoopee. Big deal."

"It *is* a big deal if you want to graduate in June."

"How about you, Ally? Promise me you'll keep up your debate schedule. Keep collecting those trophies."

"I haven't thought about debate." At the moment she felt overwhelmed, and preparing for the next tournament in January was the last thing on her mind.

"I'm in the hospital, Ally, not you."

A nurse signaled that her time was up. Alexis kissed Adam's forehead. "I'll be back tomorrow."

Deep in thought, Alexis went to the ICU waiting area, which now held several people. As she walked in the door, a teary-eyed Kelly hurried up to her. "How is he? They won't let me see him."

"You'll be able to see him once he goes into a private room. Probably tomorrow."

Wade materialized beside Kelly, saying, "Hey," and giving a little wave.

"Wade drove me," Kelly said. "I only have my learner's permit."

"It'll make Adam feel better knowing you came," Alexis said, trying to be charitable. She really wasn't in the mood to comfort Kelly.

"What's wrong with him?"

Baffled, Alexis said, "It's leukemia."

"That's what Sawyer told me, but how did Adam get it?"

"He's had it for years, but he's been in remission until now." Kelly offered a blank stare, and slowly revelation dawned on Alexis. "Didn't you know?"

Kelly shook her head, and her big blue eyes filled with tears. "No," she said. "He never said a word."

TWELVE

"I felt pretty stupid delivering the news to her, Adam. Wade said he hadn't known either." Alexis was with her brother the next morning. He'd been moved to a private room and was scheduled to begin his experimental treatments later that day. She'd gotten an excused absence from morning classes. The school faculty was being very sympathetic about Adam's hospitalization; plus, she was an excellent student who could afford to miss some classes.

"It didn't come up in conversation," Adam said. He was out of bed, sitting in a chair, still attached to an IV hanging on a wheeled pole, making him mobile. "I figured Kelly might have heard something because kids from our old middle school knew, but I guess they didn't say anything. Go figure."

"But not to say *anything* to your girlfriend—"

"It's a turnoff, Ally. I figured I had one chance with her, and dumping my medical history on her didn't seem like a good way to start a relationship. I saw it as need-to-know-only information, and when we started dating, she didn't need to know. Now give it a rest."

She was upsetting him, so she tempered her critical tone. "You've been dating her since last summer. I just figured she knew, that's all."

"Well, she didn't." He toyed with the IV line running into his arm. "How was she after you told her?"

"She had that deer caught in headlights expression."

"I need to call her." But he didn't make a move.

"You probably should. I'm going to school after lunch. I can give her a message."

"Tell her I'll call tonight. Do you think this will make a difference? I mean, do you think she'll still like me?"

Sympathy filled her. He'd worked so hard to be normal, to live a life everyone else their age took for granted. She wanted to throw her arms around her brother and tell him everything was going to work out fine. Yet she couldn't make false promises either. Why did he have to like Kelly instead of Tessa? Having Tessa as a girl-friend probably would have saved him heartache.

"If Kelly doesn't still like you, she's plain crazy," Alexis said, smiling quickly.

Adam returned her smile. He changed the subject. "How are Mom and Dad doing?"

"They look shell-shocked. Mom's shut off her phones. Dad's been coming home early from his office. It's kind of like they've circled up the wagons, know what I mean?"

"I wish they'd go back to their everyday lives. It doesn't help knowing I've turned them upside down."

"I don't miss the arguing," Alexis said. "They're upset, but not with each other. Mom wants to camp here at the hospital like she did before, though. They've had words about that."

He shook his head. "I don't want her to."

"Neither does Dad. He called her a martyr, which made her mad. I heard him tell her this was your disease, not hers."

"Then Dad gets it," Adam said. "He under-stands."

"I don't," Alexis confessed.

"It doesn't do anybody any good for Mom to live here twenty-four-seven. It may make her feel righteous, but it doesn't do anything for you and Dad."

"We'll survive. We did before."

A nurse came in to take his vital signs. "Go on to school now," he said. "I'll see you tonight."

On Saturday when Alexis went to visit Adam, she found Kelly in his room. They were sitting together at the small table. Adam wore street clothes, but he was still linked to the IV, and he had a mask over his nose and mouth.

"Hi," Kelly said, looking stiff and uncomfortable. The look of bliss in Adam's eyes lit up the room.

"Nice to see you," Alexis said, and this time she meant it. "I'd have brought you if you needed a ride."

"My dad brought me. He's downstairs in the lobby."

"Well, if you ever want to come, just call me. I come every day."

"Look what Kelly brought me." Adam held up a sports magazine.

Alexis knew he subscribed to the magazine, but evidently it was more special because Kelly had brought it. "Sports . . . now, there's a sleeping pill if I ever saw one," Alexis joked.

Kelly fidgeted with the ends of her hair.

"Kelly's been asked to be on the school dance team," Adam said, breaking an awkward silence. "Tell my sister."

"Um, yes, the captain of the dance team recommended me to Mrs. Tyner, and she's asked me to try out in January. That's when the team forms for next year."

"Excellent," Alexis said, even though she really didn't care.

"Not many sophomores are invited to try out for the team. It's mostly juniors and seniors."

"And you'll be a junior next year," Alexis pointed out. "Good timing."

After another minute of awkward silence, Kelly stood. "I should be going."

"You just got here." Adam looked crestfallen.

"Dad's waiting, and he's got other stuff to do today. I'll call you." She leaned over and hesitantly kissed his forehead. She whisked out the door with a wave.

"Gee, was it something I said?" Alexis asked.

"She was nervous. It's the first time we've seen each other since the night I passed out in front of her. And you could have been more excited about the dance team."

"Should I send flowers?"

"Ally . . . ," Adam said in a warning tone.

"Zipping my lip," Alexis said, making a sliding motion across her mouth.

Kelly's perfume lingered in the room like a ghost standing between them.

The new drugs made Adam deathly ill. He was to take the special drug cocktail by IV every day for eight days, then wait two weeks before resuming the medication. The clinical trial was to last eight weeks, and he would be closely monitored throughout. "He'll be in the hospital until January," Eleanor explained to Alexis. "He can't even come home for Christmas."

"Then we'll bring Christmas to him," Alexis said. "And Thanksgiving too."

The week before Thanksgiving, Alexis organized a pilgrim party, and with the help of her friends, cut out construction-paper turkeys, pumpkins and pilgrim hats, made paper chains in fall colors and built a large replica of the *Mayflower* from cardboard. After receiving permission from the hospital staff, they decorated the walls of the pediatric floor with the colorful shapes. On Thanksgiving day, Alexis and her friends arrived early and set up tables in the pediatric playroom for the families of kids too sick to leave the hospital. They spread paper leaves over the butcher-paper-covered tabletops and set out wicker baskets filled with trinkets and party favors as centerpieces. They filled balloons with helium, tied long ribbons to them and let them float to the ceiling. The hospital cafeteria would serve turkey with all the trimmings to the group.

"Looks great," a nurse told Alexis just before the kids and their parents arrived from their rooms for the meal. "We try to do this for the kids ourselves every year, but it's hard when we've got our own families to think about. These kids deserve something special. Thanks for taking over and doing such a nice job."

"It was fun," Alexis said. She was glad others could benefit from the effort, but it was Adam she had been thinking about. She never wanted him to spend another Thanksgiving in the hospital.

Unfortunately, because of his new treatments, Adam was too sick to eat, so he remained in his room and slept, but everyone else showed up and appeared to have a good time, including her parents. Just before the meal ended, Eleanor said, "Be right back." She soon returned carrying a large cake shaped like a fat turkey wearing a pilgrim hat. Its tail feathers were spread like a fan and colored in bright shades of frosting. The body of the turkey was dome shaped, not flat like most cakes. Individual icing feathers had been meticulously sculpted in neat rows. "Wow," one of the fathers said. "Where did you buy that?"

"I made it," she said shyly. "It's a white cake with chocolate icing and buttercream filling, my son's favorite."

All the children clustered around the cake, begging for a slice.

Alexis said, "Way to go, Mom."

Eleanor actually blushed. "I remembered how much he liked this kind of cake, so I dug through my old recipe box until I found the recipe. I took a confectionary how-to course many years ago, so I own all the decorator frosting tips and paraphernalia. And I was surprised at how quickly things came back to me once I started."

A memory stirred inside Alexis of a birthday party when she and Adam had been six. Their mother had made them twin superhero cakes—Superman for Adam, Wonder Woman for Alexis. The cakes were shaped like the characters, and their costumes were correct to the smallest detail.

Alexis had loved that party, and at the time, thought that their mom could do anything.

Eleanor cut the cake, and Blake began passing it around. "Nice work," he said with an expression on his face that Alexis hadn't seen there in ages.

Alexis took two pieces. "I'll save one for Adam. Who knows? Maybe he'll feel like eating it later."

Adam did feel better later, and he did eat the cake. "This is really good," he kept telling his mother with every bite. "I mean *really* good."

Eleanor couldn't stop smiling.

When Alexis arrived home that evening, Sawyer was parked in her driveway. "Hey," he said. "How did the big feast go?"

"Great." She walked over to his car and leaned into the driver's side window. "Everyone said they had fun. Mom baked a cake and brought it as a surprise. And boy, was I surprised! You here for a reason? All those football games can't be over already."

"They're still playing, but I thought I'd come over and make a pass at you."

"Funny," she said.

"Hop in. We'll go to a movie."

"I won't be able to stay awake."

"Come on. You can sleep in tomorrow. Unless you're planning on hitting the stores for Christmas shopping like my mom."

She hadn't even thought about Christmas shopping. "Not this year."

His eyes grew serious. "You need to get your mind off your brother, Ally."

"Are you reading my mind?"

"No," he said, running his finger along her jaw. "I'm reading your eyes. Your sad eyes."

She took a deep breath to steady the emotions that swirled through her. "It isn't fair, you know. Adam doesn't deserve this."

"I know. But he's got one terrific sister on his team."

She smiled, feeling his compliment to her bones. "All right, you win. We'll go to a movie."

He leaned across the seat and opened the passenger door. Alexis walked around the car and got in, all the while thinking about Adam shut away in a hospital, sick and in pain. No . . . it really wasn't fair at all.

At school, kids and teachers asked her about Adam, but few went to visit him. Alexis often heard the excuse "It's just too hard to see him like that." Excuses annoyed her. People were thinking about themselves, not Adam. He was lonely. He didn't say as much, but she could tell. Sometimes she'd go into his room and he'd just be sitting and staring out the window.

Of course Tessa visited him, as did Sawyer, but Kelly rarely went, and that bothered Alexis most of all. "She's supposed to be his girlfriend," Alexis fumed to Tessa. "What kind of girlfriend doesn't go to the hospital to see her boyfriend?"

"The wrong girlfriend," Tessa answered philosophically. "Bet Adam still likes her, doesn't he?"

"Talks about her all the time. But he's the one who has to call and e-mail her. She never does it first."

"I heard she's been invited to be on the dance team."

"Maybe she'll break a leg."

"Uncharitable," Tessa said. "That's not like you."

Alexis shrugged. "It's me ever since Adam got sick again. You know, the first time it happened to him, I didn't know what was going on, and that made me scared. This time I *know* what's going on, and it's making me angry." She hated both feelings but could do nothing to control either one.

One afternoon, Alexis went to visit Adam, but he wasn't in his room. She checked the playroom, the library area, the computer terminals, but he wasn't in any of those places. Just when she was growing alarmed, she turned a corner and almost plowed into him.

"Whoa. Slow down," he said. He was pushing his IV unit. A portable monitor was strapped to his chest to keep track of his heartbeat.

"Where have you been? I've been looking for you." His weight loss was more noticeable when he stood up. His clothes hung on him. Alexis made a mental note to talk to their mother about buying him new pants and shirts for Christmas.

"You found me. Too much to see and do around here," he joked. "And if you must know, I've been visiting a friend."

"You have a friend up here?" This was news to her.

He cocked his head. "Want to meet him?"

She'd half hoped it was a girl, so that he could forget about Kelly. "Sure." She followed him down a hall where she'd never been before.

"This area's for the younger kids—five and

under," he said. He stopped at a closed door, opened it a crack and said, "Hey, Rudy. It's me, Adam. Can I bring my sister in to say hi?"

A child's voice said, "Is she pretty?"

"Very pretty."

"Okay."

Adam opened the door, and Alexis peered into the semidark room. There on the bed sat a little boy. Or at least the resemblance of a little boy. For this child was a mass of scar tissue. He had no hand on one arm, a partial hand on the other. "Meet Rudy," Adam said. "He's my new buddy."

THIRTEEN

Alexis fought an automatic revulsion at Rudy's disfigurement. One side of the boy's face was horribly scarred; the other side appeared almost normal. Half of his hair was gone, and his neck looked red and raw. He wore pajamas that covered the rest of him, but she could imagine the scar tissue underneath. "Hi," she said, hoping she sounded cheerful.

"Adam says you're twins," Rudy said. His voice sounded raspy. "You don't look like twins."

"Sure we do," Adam said, moving alongside the bed with his IV pole. "Come here, Ally. Let him see the resemblance up close."

She hesitated for only a second before joining Adam. They put their cheeks together and leaned in toward Rudy. She could smell the ointment that bathed his body, but she didn't flinch. Rudy examined their faces with his good eye. "She's got hair and you don't," Rudy observed sagely. "But I guess you sort of look like each other."

Alexis pulled back, not knowing how to begin a conversation with this grossly disfigured child.

Adam came to her rescue. "My sister's won a lot of trophies."

"For sports?" Rudy asked.

"No," Alexis said. "For talking."

Rudy's one eyebrow shot up. "They give trophies for *talking?*"

His surprise was so genuine that Alexis and Adam both laughed. "It's a special kind of talking called *debating*," Alexis said.

Rudy didn't look convinced. "I have two trophies," he said, brightening. "For baseball."

"Rudy's quite the slugger," Adam said. "He played T-ball last year."

"When I get out of the hospital, I'm going out for Little League," Rudy said confidently.

The fact that he had only part of one hand didn't seem to faze him, but it brought an instant lump to Alexis's throat. "Good for you."

"I like baseball a lot."

"What position do you want to play?" she asked.

Rudy glanced up at Adam. "First base, just

like Adam. He says I can come watch him play. In the spring, right?"

Adam grinned. "That's right. Rudy's going to cheer for me."

"Where do you live?"

"Homestead." Rudy had named a city farther south, almost to the Florida Keys.

"Do you have any brothers or sisters?"

"A brother. But he's just a baby. Mom has to stay with Tony 'cause he's too little to visit me." A shadow crossed Rudy's scarred face. "Daddy drives a truck, so I don't see so much of him either."

"That's why we're friends," Adam interjected. "I told Rudy that while he's in the hospital, I'll be his big brother."

Alexis waited only a moment before asking, "So can I be your big sister?"

Rudy thought about it, and Adam leaned forward to say, "She's a pretty good sister, take it from me."

Rudy nodded. "I guess so."

Just then, a nurse stepped into the room pushing a wheelchair. "Hey, Rudy. Time for physical therapy."

He stuck out his lower lip. "I hate physical therapy. It hurts."

"No pain, no gain," Adam said. "All ballplayers have to be flexible. So they can reach for fly balls and run bases."

The nurse gave Adam a friendly wink. "You heard what Adam said. Let's get moving."

Grousing, Rudy let her help him out of the bed and into the chair. "Will you come see me later?" he asked Adam.

"Want to eat dinner together?"

Rudy agreed, and the nurse whisked him out the door.

Alexis turned toward her brother. "What happened to him?"

"A house fire. He was trapped in his room and a fireman carried him out. At first, they thought he would die. The smoke damaged his lungs and voice. He was burned badly, and he's been through a real ordeal, but the doctors pulled him through. He's been here since July. He's actually eight years old."

Alexis shivered. "Poor little boy. Why is he on this floor? I thought this was oncology."

"There's nothing but adults up in the burn unit. His doctors thought he needed to be around other kids to help him adjust. They brought him down last week."

"Will he . . . I mean, his scars . . . will they get better?"

"He's already had several skin graft operations, but no, he's always going to be scarred."

"What about the other kids? What do they say when they see him? It's quite a shock, you know, when you see him for the first time."

"He gets plenty of stares, but he's made a couple of friends down in the playroom. Can you imagine how hard it'll be for him in the real world? I guess that's one reason I made friends with him. No one should have to feel like a freak. That . . . and the fact that he's a really nice little kid." He grinned at Alexis. "I can't spend all my time lying around feeling sorry for myself, can I?"

"Never!" she said.

"That's one thing you realize about this place after you hang around for a while. No matter how bad off you think you are, there's always someone worse off." He headed toward the door, pushing the IV pole. "Come on, let's watch *Jeopardy!*"

Mrs. Wiley, the debating team coach, called Alexis up after class one afternoon in early December. "How's your brother, Alexis?"

"He's hanging in there. The new drugs really make him sick, but his doctors think they're making a difference."

"That's wonderful." She paused. "You know,

we've got a big tourney coming up in January, and you've missed several practice sessions."

"Yes, I know, and I'm sorry."

"I'm not scolding you," Mrs. Wiley added hastily. "But practice is important. We only have two more tournaments before state." She shuffled papers on her desk. "As you know, state is everything. It's why we've worked so hard. I think the team I'm taking to Tallahassee is the best I've ever coached." Only teams with the highest points went to state. Theirs had just missed by a few points when Alexis was a junior.

"I'm glad to be a part of it."

Mrs. Wiley shoved the papers aside and looked Alexis full in the face. "You're the heart of this team, Alexis. You're the one the others respect and look up to. And winning will be a gold star on your college application forms."

"I'm waiting for my SAT scores."

"You're a good student, so the SATs shouldn't hold you back. Are you still hoping to get into Stetson?"

"It's the only place I want to go," Alexis confessed, but she also knew that Stetson limited the size of its freshman class. "They get tons of applications, so they can pick and choose who they take."

"And remember, a college doesn't just look at test scores. They look at a student's overall record. They want well-balanced students, ones who can handle *all* of the college experience, not just classroom work. That's why I believe extracurricular activity is so important. Your efforts in speech and debate will be a real asset when admissions people look beyond test scores."

Slowly Alexis was catching on. Mrs. Wiley was asking Alexis to stay loyal to the team. Certainly she felt pulled and stretched in many directions, but she had never even considered quitting. "I'll be ready for the January debate," she told her teacher.

Mrs. Wiley looked relieved and offered a quick smile. "I have no doubts about your ability, Alexis, and I hope I didn't give you the wrong idea. I just know how difficult things are for you now. I want to encourage you to stay the course, so to speak."

Alexis walked out of the room feeling irritated. Did Mrs. Wiley think she couldn't handle her responsibilities just because Adam was in the hospital? If anything, she was more determined than ever to "stay the course" of her high school journey. She was doing it for herself but, in a roundabout way, for Adam too. Her experiences would become his experiences until he returned to classes himself. It was the least she could do for him, trapped in the hospital while she lived a healthy life.

When she told Tessa about the conversation after school in the library, Tessa said, "That's so unfair! Mrs. Wiley shouldn't put more pressure on you."

"I won't let the team down," Alexis insisted. "I *want* to earn points for our school. I *want* us to be champions."

"The team understands, Ally. This isn't a case of loyalty. . . . It's a matter of priority, and your brother takes priority over any debate tournament."

Tessa had put into words what was in Alexis's heart. "Tell that to Mrs. Wiley when I miss practice the next time."

Tessa grinned. "I think she's getting hyper because she's been teaching for so long and this is her own personal best shot at the top honors. She'd take your place if she could."

"You think?"

"Maybe we can buy her a long black wig and she could lose thirty pounds."

Alexis got the giggles.

Tessa banged her fist on the table like a judge

with a gavel. "Be it resolved—that teachers who coach debate for more than twenty years without winning a state trophy can substitute themselves as sacrificial lambs for the express purpose of achieving academic sainthood."

"Stop, Tessa, you're killing me."

Tessa made a goofy face. The librarian gave them a warning look.

Alexis was still in a good mood that evening as she was stepping out the door to go to the hospital. She opened the door and ran into Sawyer. "Well, hi," she said brightly. "What's up?"

"That's what I came by to ask you." He didn't look happy. "Why haven't you been answering my e-mails or phone calls?"

"I haven't turned on my computer in days. And you must not have left messages, because I don't remember any—"

"For crying out loud, Ally, how do I get a date with my own girlfriend?"

"What?" She was surprised by the vehemence in his tone.

"The Christmas dance," he said impatiently. "Are we going to the Christmas dance together or not?"

FOURTEEN

"The dance," Alexis repeated, thunderstruck. Suddenly she recalled seeing posters all over the school's common area, cafeteria and gym announcing the upcoming Snowflake Ball. Next to the prom, the ball was the biggest social event at their school, but unlike the prom, this dance was sponsored by alumni who owned businesses in the community, and it was open to the entire school. The kids often joked about it because they lived in Miami, where snowflakes never fell, and yet few wanted to miss the event. Glory and Charmaine had tried to rope her into being on the liaison committee, but she'd begged off.

"Yes, the dance," Sawyer said. "It's being advertised all over the school, you know. I just figured we'd be going, but since you've never once talked about it with me . . ."

"Sawyer . . . I—I forgot."

He looked incredulous. "What do you mean you forgot? It's next Saturday night at the downtown Hilton. Some of our friends have rented rooms for all-night parties. It's the last blowout before Christmas break."

"I didn't forget on purpose! I—I saw the posters, but I just never took time to let it sink in. Honestly, Sawyer, I didn't mean to ignore you. I—I've just got so much on my mind."

His expression softened, but still he looked perplexed. "I'm not mad at you. I know how hard it's been to have Adam in the hospital and all. It's just that, well, sometimes I feel so left out of your life. You know, like I'm some kind of afterthought. I think about you all the time, and there's no place I'd rather be than with you. It just hurts knowing you don't feel the same way."

She stiffened. "Don't lay a guilt trip on me. Please. I do think about us." She fudged some on the truth of her statement to him. Lately, she'd allowed many things to supersede thinking about Sawyer. She put her hand on his shoulder. "Do you still want to take me to the dance? I mean, I'll understand if you'd rather take your dog or something."

A small smile lifted a corner of his mouth.

"My dog already has a date for Saturday night." He looked into her eyes, as if searching for something. Finally he said, "We'll hit the dance, then go up and visit Adam, fill him in on what he didn't miss. I know you won't feel much like going to parties, so we'll skip all of them."

Relieved, Alexis put her arms around Sawyer. He had read her mind perfectly—she didn't want Adam to be all alone during a dance he'd most certainly have gone to if he'd been able. "You're wonderful."

His arms slipped around her. "No," he whispered. "Just crazy in love."

"Mom, I need a new dress." Alexis found her mother doing paperwork in her home office and broke the news. "The Snowflake Ball is in four days."

"Really? I would have thought you'd have shopped for a dress before now." Eleanor swiveled her desk chair toward Alexis.

"I forgot about it until Sawyer reminded me. Maybe I can wear a dress from last year," she added when her mother appeared distracted.

"No, no. Get a new dress. You deserve a new dress."

"Why are you looking at me that way?"

"Sorry." Her mother shook her head. "Seems sad to me that you forgot such a thing as the Snowflake Ball. It should have been on your mind for weeks. But I guess we've all had our minds on other things lately."

Alexis could tell by the expression on her mother's face that she was truly affected by Alexis's oversight, although she couldn't figure out why. "It's just a dance, Mom."

"Isn't it amazing how priorities are realigned in times of crisis?"

Alexis realized that her mother was making a comment and wasn't waiting for an answer.

"I just got off the phone with Larry Pressman," Eleanor said quietly. "He wants to appoint me to a highly visible land-use committee—sort of a reward, I think, for all the work I did for him during the campaign."

Alexis's heart skipped a beat. Being together as a family during the past several weeks had been good for all of them, regardless of the terrible circumstances. "Well, I'm sure it will help out when you run for office next year," she said, hoping her voice didn't betray her disappointment.

"That's what Larry said."

"When do you start?"

Eleanor's eyes went soft and unfocused. "I won't start. I told him no, thank you. The whole political thing . . . it's just not so important to me anymore. We don't know what's going to happen to Adam, if the drugs will work or not."

Alexis bristled. "Of course they'll work. He's already doing better." Abruptly, she asked, "Mom, would you like to help me shop for that dress?"

Her mother looked surprised. "I would have thought you'd want Tessa to go with you."

Alexis shook her head. "Tessa's not going to the dance. The only guy she cares about likes someone else, and I don't want to make her feel any worse by dragging her dress shopping with me."

"I see," Eleanor said. "Pity . . . I like Tessa. She's smart, talented and funny. Too bad this young man doesn't see that."

"Go figure," Alexis said with a shrug.

Eleanor pushed up from her chair. "Look, why don't we go poke around in some boutiques right now for that dress? We can call your father and have him meet us for dinner, then go up to the hospital and visit Adam together." She grabbed her purse and rummaged for her car keys.

Alexis didn't hesitate a second. "I'm out the door already."

"Great dress," Tessa said the next afternoon when she came home from school with Alexis. Alexis hadn't planned to show it to her, but Tessa had insisted.

"The dance is highly overrated," Alexis said.

Tessa stroked the satin fabric. "Only to girls who get invited," she said.

"Tessa, I don't want to go. It's Sawyer who wants me to go."

"Well, then you should go. And stop feeling sorry for me. If I can't go with someone I really want to go with, why go?"

Alexis walked the dress over to the closet and hung it up. "Good point. What will you do on Saturday night?"

"I can always go visit a sick friend."

Alexis smiled and returned to where Tessa was sitting on the floor. "That's a plan."

"You don't suppose Kelly will be up there with him, do you?"

"I doubt it. She hardly ever goes to see him."

"But he still likes her, doesn't he?"

" 'Fraid so." Alexis couldn't lie to her best friend. "One of life's mysteries, if you ask me."

"It does seem that the meaner a girl treats a guy, the more he wants her."

Alexis winced, because she could apply that formula to her and Sawyer too. She certainly didn't intend to treat him badly, or to be thoughtless, but she knew she was. She told herself that once Adam got out of the hospital, she was going to treat Sawyer with the kindness and consideration he deserved. "Sawyer and I will go to the dance, but we'll skip the parties and head up to the hospital. Maybe we'll run into you."

"It could happen," Tessa said, mimicking Kelly's wide-eyed innocent look.

That Friday afternoon, Alexis found Adam in Rudy's room playing cards. Rudy used a curved, slotted piece of wood to hold his cards upright, painstakingly inserting each card with his damaged fingers. Alexis was impressed by how well he was adapting to his loss and was beginning to think maybe he'd wield a bat one day too.

Once, when she and Adam had stopped by Rudy's room, they had met the fireman who had rescued him. The man was big and muscular with hands as large as ham hocks, but when he had turned to leave, Alexis had seen that his eyes glittered with tears. "You hang in there, buddy," the fireman had said.

And when he was gone, Rudy's eyes shone. "He saved me. He picked me up off the floor and carried me to my mama. He's a hero."

"You're the hero," Adam told Rudy.

The boy scrunched his face. "No way. What did I do?"

"You lived," Adam said. "And you're working hard to get well. Only heroes do that."

"If you say so. Can you and Alexis stay and play fish with me?"

At the time, Alexis had been thinking about the ton of homework waiting for her at home. But she had dragged chairs to the side of Rudy's bed, handed Adam a deck of cards and said, "Deal."

Today's card game wasn't going well because Alexis could see that Adam didn't have his mind on it. When he threw down an eight, Rudy exclaimed, "Hey! No fair. I just put down an eight and you told me to go fish."

Adam picked up the card and handed it over. "Sorry . . . guess I wasn't thinking clearly."

Alexis wondered what was bothering her brother. That was the trouble with her twin radar—it only alerted her to the presence of a problem, not the nature of the problem. When the game was finally over, they said goodbye to Rudy, and she walked with Adam, pushing his IV pole to his room. Once there, she closed the door. "What's wrong?"

Adam slumped into a chair. "What? Is my optimism waning?"

"Let's just say that your unhappiness is showing." She crouched in front of his chair, took one of his hands. "What's going on, Adam? You're not yourself. Is it . . . I mean, how are the treatments going?" Asking the question caused a shiver of fear to pass through her.

"Is that what you think? It isn't always about the cancer, Ally. I'm more than just a case of cancer, you know."

Chastised, she asked, "Then what? Rudy? Bad cafeteria food?"

Adam ignored her attempted joke. "It's Kelly," he said at last. "She . . . she called last night. She dumped me."

FIFTEEN

"Kelly dumped you?"

"As in *adiós*, see you around, don't call me, I'll call you."

Furious, Alexis cried, "How could she? How dare she!"

"She hemmed and hawed around it, but finally she just came right out and said, 'I want to date other people.'"

"What other people? Who does she want to date?"

"That's what I asked her, but she said no one in particular. She just wanted her freedom."

"Oh, that's rich."

"It's not like we were engaged or anything." Adam's voice quavered, and he cleared his throat.

"But everybody knew she was your girlfriend ever since last summer."

"I can't blame her. What girl wants a boyfriend who can't take her out on dates? Or see her at school? Or even buy her a hamburger? It's like I'm in jail."

"Well, I blame her. You're sick," Alexis said. "It isn't your fault." She stood and began pacing the room, seething inside.

"Look at me, Ally. I'm a freak. No hair. Sores all over my body from the drugs. I look like a refugee in my clothes. I'm disgusting. No girl wants to be stuck with a guy like me."

"But that's on the outside. You don't love a person for what he looks like. You love him for what he *is*."

Adam gave a derisive laugh. "Get real. Looks matter, and you know it. Why are you so upset? You never liked her anyway."

"But *you* liked her. She had no right to break it off with you when you can't do anything to win her back."

"Well, she's gone," he said. "She's free to be with whomever she wants." He sagged in his chair like a rag doll. The energy had gone out of him, and tears swam in his eyes.

Alexis thought her heart would break for him. "She shouldn't have treated you this way," she said under her breath. "What kind of a person kicks someone when they're down?"

Alexis dressed slowly and meticulously for the dance. She figured she owed it to Sawyer to look her best. And she figured she owed it to herself for when she nailed Kelly to the wall. There was no way she was getting off scot-free.

"Are you sure she'll be at the dance?" Tessa had asked when Alexis told her on the phone what had happened.

"She'll be there, all right. There's no doubt in my mind. Why else would she have used that line about dating other people?"

"Gee, I'm sorry I'm going to miss the fire-works. Does Sawyer know?"

"I'll fill him in, but he's not going to talk me out of dealing with her."

"Should I have the police standing by?"

"Not necessary. It'll be a clean kill."

"What about teacher chaperones? I don't want you to get in trouble."

"I'm a senior in good standing, remember? What are they going to do to me—keep me from graduating because I tie some dopey little sopho-more into knots?"

"Ah, but a sophomore who's on the dance team," Tessa reminded her.

"What's that got to do with anything?"

"Nothing. Just thought I'd remind you that she does have friends."

"Name two."

Tessa was silent. "All right, people tolerated her because she was Adam's girlfriend."

"And now she isn't. She's fair game."

"I know you're protecting your brother, Ally, but don't get too carried away. Will you promise me?"

Alexis sighed. "All right, I won't draw blood, okay?"

"Well, if you do, just make sure you don't get any on that fabulous satin dress of yours."

For the first time that night, Alexis laughed. Trust Tessa to break the tension. "I'll be careful," she said. *Very careful.*

The Hilton ballroom glowed with light from sparkling crystal chandeliers. Oversized glittering snowflakes hung from the ceiling over a sea of linen-topped dining tables, and buffet tables were draped with royal blue cloths set with silver platters and elegant tureens. A dance floor of smooth black marble shone at one end of the enormous room, which was fronted by a stage where a live band played.

"Do you think they're going to play that Muzak stuff all night?" Sawyer asked, picking a cheese cube off a platter.

Alexis was too busy surveying the ballroom full of her classmates to care about the music. "Maybe they'll change it after we eat," she said.

"Hope so. They need to pick up the pace." He took several more cheese cubes and tossed them into his mouth like candy. "Have I mentioned that you look good enough to eat?"

"Twice, and thank you."

He followed her gaze around the room. "You still looking for the little traitor?"

She focused on Sawyer. "I know she's here. I just have to locate her."

"What are you going to do? Throw her into the ambrosia salad?"

"Very funny. I just want to talk to her. What she did to Adam was cruel and thoughtless. You don't break up with your boyfriend the day before a huge dance that he can't take you to through no fault of his own."

"But you've never liked her. I'd have thought you'd be glad she and Adam were history. Why do you care?"

"Because Adam cares."

"So if somebody tromped all over me the way Kelly did him, would you flatten her for my sake?"

He was leaning against the table, his arms crossed, looking hunky in a white dinner jacket. Alexis patted his cheek. "That's a trick question and you know it."

"How so?"

"Because you're big and strong. And healthy. You can take care of yourself."

"But if I couldn't?"

She leaned forward and kissed his cheek. "Then I'd clobber her."

He grinned. "The old 'Hurt me, but don't lay a finger on someone I love.' Is that it?"

"Sort of."

"So that must mean you love me."

She laughed. "What am I going to do with you?"

All of a sudden, Sawyer, looking over Alexis's head, straightened and said, "Traitor alert."

Alexis whipped around. "Where?" But the question was unnecessary. She saw Kelly immediately. The girl wore a long silvery dress that clung to her every curve, and her long white-blond hair hung like a curtain of light down her bared back.

Alexis felt her pulse quicken. Beside Kelly, dressed in a black tux, stood Wade. *Two traitors.* Somehow she wasn't surprised.

"Now what?" Sawyer asked.

"Now we wait," Alexis said.

Alexis bided her time, waiting until she saw Kelly head off to the ladies' room. "Be right back," she told Sawyer.

"Fifteen minutes," he said, "then I'm coming in after you."

Because it was early in the evening, the ladies' lounge wasn't filled with girls primping at the mirrors. Only Kelly. That was where Alexis found her when she went in. The second Kelly saw Alexis, the color drained from her face. Alexis shot her daggers in the mirror while she walked up behind her.

"Please don't hate me," Kelly said in a little-girl voice.

"Why shouldn't I? You hurt my brother. If he'd been a regular guy and you dumped him, I'd have told him to suck it up and move on. But he's not a regular guy, and you know that."

Kelly's gaze darted away from Alexis's withering stare. "I tried really hard to be Adam's girlfriend. . . . I really did— I mean, I *do* like him, but I just can't take the sick part."

"How do you know? You almost never went to visit him!"

"Don't yell at me," Kelly pleaded. "I wanted to stick by him. I really did. But . . . but whenever I saw him, I just fell apart. Don't you think I'm hurt over this too?"

"You look wounded, and so does Wade," Alexis said coldly. "So ready to step in and help you over your pain."

"Don't hate Wade because of me. Neither of us wanted to hurt Adam, but we just started liking each other. We couldn't help it."

"Was it all just a game to you, Kelly? Did you just fake caring about Adam?"

"I liked Adam just fine. It was fun being the girlfriend of a popular senior," Kelly said defensively. "I—I liked that part. But not the other part. I just can't stand seeing him melt away, and I don't think I should have to apologize because I've moved on. I'm sorry I'm not strong enough for you, Alexis. I'm sorry I don't measure up to your standards."

Alexis wanted to shake the girl until her teeth rattled, but she knew it would accomplish nothing. Emotionally, Kelly was like a shallow pond. In a storm of adversity, she had no depth, and therefore no place to anchor her loyalty. She could be no safe harbor for someone who loved her. "Kelly, you're pathetic. I feel sorry for you because you don't know that love and loyalty go together. Just remember, what you dish out will one day come back to you. You and Wade deserve each other."

Alexis turned on her heels and left the ladies' room.

Sawyer was leaning against a wall, waiting for her out in the hallway.

"Kelly's sorry, but it's just too painful for her to watch Adam suffer." Alexis boiled down the confrontation into one burst of anger, dripping with sarcasm.

Sawyer pushed off from the wall, took her arm. "Time to go."

Hot tears of frustration brimmed in Alexis's eyes. "I shouldn't be making you leave."

"The music sucks. Come on. Let's go see your brother." He slipped her sweater around her shoulders, and together they walked out of the ballroom.

Adam was listlessly flipping through TV channels when they arrived in his room. "Short dance," he said, looking surprised to see them.

"We didn't want to stay," Alexis said. "The air stunk."

"Who was she with?"

"Wade," Sawyer said. "Want me to break his kneecaps for you?"

Adam grinned halfheartedly. "You can't make somebody love you if they don't. I guess I always knew Kelly was with me for the wrong reasons."

Alexis didn't mention her talk with Kelly. Why prolong Adam's misery? "You want company?" she asked.

"You two are dressed up. Go out and have a good time."

Sawyer picked up the remote and aimed it at the TV. "I think there's a game on ESPN. What's more fun than watching that?"

"Watching paint dry?" Alexis asked.

Sawyer snorted and exchanged pity-the-poor-girl looks with Adam.

They were just settling in when Tessa swooped into the room, carrying two brown grocery sacks. "It's me, a *geek* bearing gifts," she joked at her own expense.

"What are you doing here?" Adam asked.

In the turmoil of the evening, Alexis had forgotten Tessa's statement about dropping by to visit a sick friend.

"I was bored stupid at home, so I said to

myself, 'Self, why not get out of here and do something fun?' "

"Coming here is fun?" Adam asked. "You've got to get out more often."

"Let me help," Sawyer said, taking one of the sacks. He put it on the table.

"What's in the bags?" Adam asked.

To Alexis, he sounded more like his old self, and she silently blessed Tessa for taking his mind and heart off Kelly.

Tessa seized the remote from Sawyer and turned off the television. "I've brought good stuff." She opened a bag and proceeded to pull out board games one by one. "I've got Clue, Trivial Pursuit, Monopoly, Scrabble—a game for every taste and every mood. And if that's not enough . . ." She reached into the bag again and brought out dominoes, checkers and three decks of cards. "Plus, for those of us who hanker for a little snack while we play"—she reached into the second bag—"I've brought popcorn, soda, a bag of M&Ms, a can of peanuts, two packages of Oreos, one package of Vienna Fingers and *ta-dum*, a thermos full of rocky road ice cream."

"All right!" Sawyer said, taking the lid off the Monopoly box. "What say we team up, Adam, and take on these two amateurs?"

"Are we being challenged?" Alexis asked Tessa. "The debate queens of Kendall High?"

"Seems so," Tessa said, stacking up the Monopoly money.

Adam pulled his chair closer to the table. "I'm already a winner," he said, glancing appreciatively from face to face. "Thanks to you three, I just got a Get Out of Jail Free card without even rolling the dice."

SIXTEEN

"It's official. I'm stuck here for Christmas," Adam told Alexis. He was in bed that day because he was having a particularly difficult time with his treatments. The chemo cocktail had taken its toll, leaving him limp, weak, without any energy. He kept a bedpan within reach because he could keep nothing in his stomach.

"Can't you bribe your doctor to let you out for one day?" Alexis was in his room addressing Christmas card envelopes for their mother, who'd gone down to buy the two of them some lunch. School was out for the holidays, and they came to visit Adam every day.

"I've already begged," Adam said.

The pediatric floor was decorated for the holidays, but the number of patients staying over the holidays was going to be small. Of those who were staying, a few would receive day passes, enabling them to leave on Christmas Eve and return late afternoon on Christmas Day. But not Adam.

"Well, not to worry. I've already got a plan."

"Ally, you always have a plan."

"It's a good plan. We're going to set up an artificial tree in that corner"—she pointed—"and bring all our gifts down here first thing Christmas morning. How's that sound?"

"It sounds like I'll be the only one in the family without presents to give."

"*Au contraire,*" Alexis said with a wave of her hand. "I took the liberty of shopping for you. You bought Dad a bookstore gift card, Mom a sweater with fake fur trim and me two new CDs. Thanks a bunch."

He shook his head. "Gee, I hardly remembering hitting the stores. Did I have fun picking out these things?"

"Tessa and I acted on your behalf, so yes, you had fun."

"Well, is it too late to ask you to do me a favor?"

She laid down her ballpoint pen. Even from where she was sitting, she could see that Adam was struggling with the exertion of talking. His skin had a yellow cast, and purplish half circles lay under his eyes like bruises. "Anything, just name it," she said.

"I've heard that Rudy's finally going home."

"Wow, that's a great Christmas present."

"Yes, it is. And I thought of another one. I lie here with plenty of time to think," he said. "Nights are the worst because I wake up and can't get back to sleep."

"Did you tell Mom? Or your doctor?"

He took a couple of deep breaths. "This isn't about sleeping better. It's about something I want to do for him. And for the other kids too. But I'll need your help."

"Tell me what you want."

"Maybe it's something you and Tessa can do together. I know how much you both like projects."

"I'm sure Tessa will help."

"You'll have to get money from Dad."

"Piece of cake."

A tiny smile quivered on his mouth. "Then here's what I want you to do for me. . . ."

With less than a week before Christmas, Alexis picked up Tessa for their day of special shopping from the list Adam had given her. "He wants *me* to help?" Tessa asked. "I can't get over it."

"He asked that we do it together. And why shouldn't he? You visit him almost as much as I do. He's depending on you. That should tell you something about his feelings for you."

"It tells me that I'm like a second sister to him," Tessa said. "Not that I'm complaining. Although I'd rather have him look at me with love in his eyes. You know, the way Sawyer looks at you."

"All in good time," Alexis said. It heartened Alexis to know that Tessa saw past Adam as he was now, ravaged by cancer and his treatments. "Ready to hit the stores?"

"Are we financed?"

Alexis reached into her purse and pulled out a small square of plastic. "Dad's card."

"He's given it to you again? *After* Disney World?"

To Alexis, the days at Disney were a distant memory. So much had happened since then. "Not for me. For Adam," she said, putting the car into gear.

They went to three department stores, four specialty stores and two giant toy stores, where they looked at more than a hundred different teddy bears before choosing the ones they wanted. "The most important ingredient," Tessa said, stroking one of the cute, cuddly bears as Alexis wove in and out of the heavy holiday traffic.

Next they went to a party store, where they bought several bags of party favors. And finally, they stopped at a piece-goods store and bought an assortment of material, sequins, glue, thread and other odds and ends. After five hours of shopping, they returned to Alexis's house and spread their bounty out on the dining room table. "The most underused piece of furniture in the place," Alexis told Tessa. She wasn't complaining, because she and her parents ate most of their meals up at the hospital these days as a family.

They began to sort through the party favors and were cutting pieces of material into heart and star shapes when Eleanor came into the room. "What are the two of you up to?"

"A very special project," Alexis said, snipping away at a yard of red satin. "Adam wants to give every kid on his floor a teddy bear for Christmas. Especially Rudy. But he doesn't want them to be just store-bought teddy bears. He wants each one to be customized for its owner. Clever, huh?"

"How many bears are we talking about?"

Eleanor scanned the table strewn with fuzzy bear bodies of different shapes and sizes.

"Fifteen."

"And the two of you are going to customize *fifteen* bears by Christmas?"

"By Christmas Eve," Alexis said. "That's when Adam wants to take them around to every room and give them away."

"How do you know what's special to these kids? How do you know how to customize these bears?"

"Adam's made friends with everyone on the floor, and he's written down what each kid likes best. All we have to do is follow the list he's made and tag the bear with the child's name." She held up a page of notes.

"This one's for Rudy," Tessa said, lifting a soft brown potbellied bear from the table. A fireman's hat was strapped to its head, and a party-favor-sized ax was tied to its paw. "Don't you think he's adorable? We're thinking of gluing a red satin heart onto his chest too. Or maybe a yellow satin star with HERO written on it. What do you think would look better?"

Eleanor stroked the bear, fingering the hat and the assortment of hearts and stars spread out like a fan. "Adam thought of this?"

"He did," Alexis said. She watched her mother's eyes go misty.

Eleanor cleared her throat. "Can I help?"

"Absolutely," Alexis said without hesitation. "Neither Tessa nor I can sew worth a darn, and we'd really rather sew the heart or star on than glue it."

"I can sew. I used to make your little dresses, remember?" Eleanor pulled out a dining room chair and began to thread a needle. "I like the star idea better," she said. "More boyish, don't you think?"

Alexis and Tessa exchanged glances. "Sure, Mom. Knock yourself out. There's plenty of sewing to do."

When Alexis's father came home, he stopped in the doorway of the dining room, and Alexis once more explained about the project.

"Pretty ambitious," he said. "A different bear for every kid?"

"It's a good idea," Alexis insisted. "Although I think it would be a good thing to give bears away to *every* child the minute he or she's admitted to the floor. Of course, they couldn't be customized, but the child would have something soft to hug."

"You're right," Eleanor said. "Something cuddly to hug would be nice. I remember how scared

Adam was when he was first checked in at age eleven. He was probably too old for teddy bears, but I know that if someone had handed him one he would have held on to it."

Alexis thought back to that time when everything had changed for her family, and she wanted to say that things can be pretty scary for kids left alone at home too. "People are never too old for teddy bears. I still have my old Winnie the Pooh bear in my closet."

Her father set down his briefcase and walked around the table to stand beside her mother. "What are you working on?"

Eleanor held up her handiwork for his inspection. "A ballerina bear. See the little toe shoes? We made them out of felt. And I sprinkled glitter on her tutu."

"It's for Sara," Alexis said, looking over at the list. "She's nine, and she has leukemia."

Her father examined the bear, then handed it back to his wife. "Nice job. I'd forgotten how well you sew."

"I haven't done it for years, but I used to love sewing. I'd forgotten just how much."

He gently swiped his thumb down her cheek. "You have glitter stuck to your skin."

"It'll wash off."

He peered over at Alexis. "Is there anything I can do to help?"

Surprised by her father's offer, she thought quickly. "How about ordering in some pizza? We're starved."

"I can handle that," he said, sounding pleased.

"And then we're going to need some name tags. Maybe you can make some on the computer with a couple of cool typefaces. I'll punch a hole in the corners and tie them to each bear with a ribbon. Here's the list of names we'll need."

He saluted her and took the piece of paper she handed him. "I'm on my way."

Alexis caught Tessa's eye and shrugged. Who could have guessed that either of her parents would want to work on dressing up teddy bears for sick kids? Certainly not her.

Adam grinned like a kid who'd won a prize when Alexis, Tessa and his parents brought the box full of bears to his room two days before Christmas. He examined every bear, proclaimed each perfect and listened wholeheartedly while they took turns explaining how they'd made each one.

"Besides paying for it, what did you do, Dad?"

"I made tags and invested a small fortune in

pizza and Chinese food. The worker bees needed nourishment, you know."

"I don't want to wait until tomorrow," Adam said. "Let's deliver them right now."

When his parents went to get a wheelchair from the nurses' station, he asked Alexis, "They got into this without you begging them?"

"Totally into it. I was shocked by how into it they got."

Tessa said, "I think they were disappointed that we only had to make fifteen."

"Whatever. I'm glad they wanted to help," Adam said. "What should we call the project? Bears this cute should have a name, don't you think?"

"How about Adam's Bears?" Alexis offered. "Short and to the point."

"Too boring." He snapped his fingers. "How about Boo-Boo Bears?"

"Adam's Boo-Boo Bears," Tessa amended. "Their owners should know who masterminded the goodies."

As soon as their parents returned with the wheelchair, Adam climbed in and settled his mask over his nose and mouth, a Santa hat on his head and the box of bears on his lap. Alexis and Tessa pushed him along the hall and into every room, where he doled out each custom-made bear to its intended owner. Every child was thrilled, and Alexis knew that part of their delight was because the gift had come from Adam, because he cared, because he'd befriended them.

Adam saved Rudy's room for last. "I'll wait in the hall," Tessa said.

Once inside, Adam handed Rudy his fireman bear and a wrapped package that had been at the bottom of the delivery box. Alexis had not seen it until that moment, and she gave Adam a questioning look, which he politely ignored. "Merry Christmas, little brother."

"Both presents are for *me?*"

"Sure are."

Rudy hugged the bear and pronounced it "awesome," then sat it on the bed so he could tear into the package. "Wow," he said, removing Adam's old baseball glove. "Is it real?"

Alexis felt her breath catch.

"It's real, and it's already broken in," Adam said. "You're the only brother I'll ever have, and I want you to keep it. You take good care of it, hear?"

"I will!" Rudy's eyes shone in his scarred face.

"You have a merry Christmas," Adam said. "And call me and tell me what Santa brings you."

When they were again in the hall, Alexis said, "Why did you do that?"

"It needs a good home. I had Dad wrap it up because I knew you'd try and talk me out of giving it away."

"But—"

"No, Ally. This is what I want. If things work out and I get to play in the spring, you can buy me a new one, okay?"

She nodded, not trusting herself to speak.

Adam leaned back in the chair, looked up at Alexis and Tessa. "I think the bears were a real hit. Now I know how Santa Claus feels. Thanks for making it happen."

"Well, Santa's elves here are worn out. Look at this." Alexis held out her hands. "Chipped nails, and glue stuck to my skin. It may never come off."

Adam's eyes crinkled around the mask, and Alexis knew he was smiling. "I don't think elves whine and complain. They're happy and cheerful."

"Ha! That's what you think. Next year we're forming a union for the humane treatment of elves and other Christmas helpers."

Adam pressed his forefingers to his temples. "Let's see. . . . Tell me, sis, can you read my mind right now about what I think of your proposed elf union?"

She feigned shock. "Of course I can, and what you're thinking is positively *rude*, Adam Chappel. Especially for Santa Claus."

He laughed heartily, and the sound warmed her heart.

SEVENTEEN

In mid-January, Adam's doctors allowed him to come home. On the Friday afternoon he checked out, Tessa pulled Alexis aside and said, "He doesn't look so good. Are you sure he should be getting out of here?"

Alexis dismissed her friend's concerns. "They wouldn't let him go if he wasn't better. I remember when he came home the other two times. He was sick, but after a few weeks, he got stronger, and then he did everything again. He just needs some time. He'll be fine."

Adam was restricted to the house. He was to go to the hospital for outpatient lab workups weekly, with the understanding that if his doctors didn't like what they saw, he would be re-admitted. Alexis assumed that her brother would chafe against the confinement, but Adam was too weak, too sick to do much more than remain in bed.

Eleanor put a bell on Adam's bedside table, telling him, "If you want anything, ring it. I'm just downstairs."

"Just until you get your strength back," his father told him.

"We can always put a hospital bed in the living room if you'd like to be downstairs," Eleanor suggested.

Adam looked horrified. "I want to stay in my room. I'll feel like I'm on display in the living room." He stopped and glanced up at Eleanor, looking contrite. "Course, that means you'll have to run up the stairs all day long."

"I don't mind. It'll keep me fit."

Without daily visits to the hospital, Alexis had assumed that her time would be freer. She was wrong. With a full class load, she faced tests and papers she'd put off all year. In March, Mrs. Wiley stepped up debate rehearsals to three afternoons a week because their team had barely squeaked out a win at the last tournament before state. "We're going in as top seed," she kept saying if anyone complained. "Only a few more weeks, so hang in there. We can win the whole enchilada. I know we can."

With so much of her time and energy going to home and school, Alexis had little time for other things. Especially for Sawyer.

With only a week remaining before she was to leave for Tallahassee, he stopped by the house. He looked grimy from soccer practice, and she figured he'd come straight from the field. "Mom's at the store, and Adam's asleep," she said. "Come up to my room and we'll talk."

"I never see you anymore," he said, looking unhappy and getting right to the point once they were upstairs.

"We see each other. I'm at school every day."

"With your face in a book. How about showing up at a few of my soccer games?" His season was in full swing. The team played once a week after school, but she rarely went.

"You know I have a ton of work. Mrs. Wiley is smelling that championship, and she's like a dog with a bone. I have to do my best; there will be a ton of college recruiters there. You should understand about that. Don't coaches come watch you play? Aren't you trying for a soccer scholarship?"

"You know I am, but I don't want to sacrifice you and me."

"Are you saying I do?"

They had squared off and were standing in the middle of her room facing each other.

"I'm just asking for a little more time with my girl. I get the stuff about school and debate, even though it never used to string you out like this. But why don't we ever have any extra time with each other? Not even on weekends?"

"You know I tutor Adam," Alexis said. "He's having a hard time getting his strength up."

"He's on the homebound program. He has teachers."

"He does, but if he's going to graduate in June with our class, he needs a lot more help than he's getting. He's sick almost every day, so the window on working with him is short."

Sawyer looked exasperated. "Why are you putting this on yourself, Ally? You're not responsible for whether or not he graduates in June."

"I want to walk with my brother. We started first grade together. I want us to finish high school together. What's so hard to understand about that?" She was becoming impatient with Sawyer.

"Don't turn me into some insensitive clod just because I want to spend time with you."

"And don't you turn me into a uncaring pain because I have more on my mind than you."

"Well, gee, Ally, forgive me for being so narrow-minded and thoughtless. Don't you think I get it? I know how important Adam is to you. But what about us? Where is the *us* in the picture these days?"

"Don't make me choose, Sawyer."

He grabbed his jacket, which he'd tossed on her bed. "You already have," he said.

Totally stunned by Sawyer's vehemence, Alexis watched him go, heard him bound down the stairs and heard the front door shut hard behind him. After the heat of the fight, the air grew quiet until all she heard was her own breathing. A moment later, Adam's bell rang. She went to his room quickly. "Do you need something?" Her voice quavered.

"Did I just hear you and Sawyer going at it?"

"Sorry if we woke you."

"I don't care about that. I wasn't eavesdropping, but it didn't sound like the two of you were hugging and kissing."

"We had a fight because he doesn't think I'm spending enough time with him." She edged into a chair. "I told him to take a number and get in line."

"Don't do that to him, Ally. He's crazy about you."

"What's the use? We're going off to separate colleges, so we'll have to break up sooner or later anyway. Why put off the inevitable?"

"Listen to me—you should put off the inevitable as long as you can. Take it from someone who knows."

"What's that supposed to mean?"

"I've just spent the last few months putting off the inevitable, but I can't do it much longer."

She felt as if he'd stabbed her. "Don't talk about—"

"What? Dying? Why can't anybody use that word around here? Am I the only one who can say it out loud?"

"Stop it." She stood, irritated that he'd needle her this way. "You're not going to die."

He closed his eyes, waited a minute. When he opened his eyes, he said quietly, "My liver's failing. I go every week for tests, and that's what the tests show. The meds they gave me have destroyed my liver. They can't fix it."

She wanted to put her hand across his mouth to stop the flow of his terrible words. "What are you saying? How could they give you drugs that hurt you?"

"Because they'd given me everything else and nothing worked. I knew the new drugs were risky—they told me so from my first consultation in the hospital. I took the risk anyway because it was also my only chance. I thought you knew."

"No one told me about the risks."

"Look, I—I didn't mean for you to *not* know. It wasn't a secret. I thought Mom and Dad explained it to you."

"No one told me," she repeated, feeling as if he'd hammered her with powerful body blows. Why hadn't she known? Why hadn't someone told her the truth? "That's not right. . . ." She couldn't decide which of the two was worse for her, the not knowing about the true potential of the drugs to harm him, or the fact that no one had been open and honest with her about his chances of survival.

"I wore a heart monitor," Adam said gently. "I was constantly tested. What did you think was going on?"

"You were sick the last time you were treated. All the chemo made you sick. I thought this was the same thing." Her voice had faded to a whisper, and her face felt hot.

"I relapsed twice. Medical science was all out of options. And now, so am I."

She couldn't see his face clearly for the tears in her eyes.

"Hey, hey, don't cry for me. I'm okay with this. We all have to die sometime. Someone has to go first, big sister."

"Don't say that to me! You're doing your schoolwork. You're going to graduate with me."

He reached out his hand, but she wouldn't take it. "I'm doing everything I can to keep that date with you. I want to make it. I really do. I just can't promise you I will."

She couldn't speak. She couldn't even feel. She was numb all over. She left Adam's room without a word, easing the door shut behind her.

"Why are you sitting alone in the dark?" Eleanor asked, coming into the living room.

Alexis was curled into a fetal position on the sofa, and she didn't answer.

Her mother set a bag of groceries on the coffee table. "Honey, what is it?" Alexis heard her breath catch. "Adam—?"

"He's asleep," Alexis said.

Eleanor leaned over, turned on a lamp, then sat on the edge of the sofa. She stroked Alexis's shoulder, but Alexis recoiled. "Don't touch me."

"Honey, what's wrong?"

"Adam's going to die and nobody saw fit to tell me." She aimed her words like darts. "The drugs that were supposed to save him are killing him."

Her mother blew out a full breath of air in one long weary sigh. "Cancer's killing him," she corrected Alexis. "We were out of options. We talked it over. He wanted to go with the experimental treatments."

"Why didn't someone ask *me*? Aren't I a part of this family? Don't I get a say?"

"What would you have said, Ally?"

She was struck dumb, because she knew she would have made the same choice they had. Every day of life Adam had earned from the experimental drugs had been a gift to all of them. Every single day.

Her mother said, "We didn't keep it from you on purpose. I—I guess I thought you'd figure it out."

"Figure it out?" Alexis sat up, unable to believe her mother was saying such a stupid thing to her. "How should I have gone about figuring out that my brother was dying right in front of me?"

Eleanor pressed her thumb and forefinger against her eyes, rocked back and forth. "Maybe I could have sat you down for a heart-to-heart talk. But frankly, your optimism, your irrepressible sense of hope, your projects, your energy were infectious. It kept us all going."

"Don't you mean my stupidity?"

Eleanor eased off the sofa. "Can I show you something?" She went over to the bookcase, pulled out a book and returned. "Do you know what this is?"

No answer.

"It's your and Adam's baby book. I want to tell you some things, and I want you to listen, not just with your ears, but with your heart."

EIGHTEEN

Alexis moved over, but she was careful not to let her mother touch her. She was angry and she was hurt, and she didn't feel like pretending otherwise. She wasn't going to be patient and understanding. Not this time. Still, her gaze was drawn to the oversized book her mother held. It was bound between covers of padded moiré satin in a soft shade of yellow. The title, *It's Twins!* was printed in blue in a fancy typeface that looked like ribbon unfurling.

"I did a good job of keeping this up," Eleanor said. "Until the two of you were about three. Then . . . well, you kept me pretty busy and I put it aside. I found it again right after Thanksgiving, and I spent hours going over every page."

She opened the book and Alexis saw two hospital bracelets: one pink, with the words FEMALE

CHAPPEL written on it, the other blue, bearing
MALE CHAPPEL. On the facing page, she read her
own and Adam's names, birth weights and vital
statistics written in their mother's neat hand. She
refused to speak.

"I was shocked when my doctor told me I was
having twins," Eleanor said. "During the last six
weeks of my pregnancy, I was confined to bed
because you two wanted out prematurely. I
wanted you out too, but once you got out, your
father and I thought we'd lose our minds."
Eleanor gave a little laugh. "We had the nursery
all fixed up with two of everything—two cribs,
two dressers, two diaper pails—the list goes on.
But every time we put you in separate cribs, you
screamed your heads off. Adam was worse than
you. He was inconsolable and could cry for hours.
Your father and I took turns sleeping and walking
the floors with you, trying to make you happy.
Then one night, in desperation, I put Adam in
your crib facing you, and he stopped crying.

"Your father and I slept that night like we
hadn't slept in weeks. When we got up the next
morning, the two of you were asleep and your
arms were around each other. I think that's all
either of you wanted, just to be together. You
shared the same crib until you were three months

old. Then we put the cribs side by side, so that you could see each other last thing at night and first thing when you woke up in the morning."

Alexis didn't need her mother to tell her how close she and Adam had been as children. She had memories of her own, just not ones that went that far back.

Eleanor flipped through the pages of the baby book filled with Alexis and Adam's shared history. "You always had the magic touch with him, Ally. You seemed to know what he wanted when he cried. When the two of you were toddlers and he'd cry, you'd get up, waddle over to the toy box and bring him just the thing that would make him stop crying. If *I* tried to guess what he wanted, he'd throw whatever I gave him on the floor and yell louder."

"But then he got sick." Alexis finally broke her silence.

"Yes. And I all but lived at the hospital with him, while you and your father fended for yourselves."

"I missed you both." Feelings of loss bubbled up within her. She remembered the ache as clearly as if it had all happened yesterday.

"I know. So did your father. But I felt so responsible for keeping Adam alive. I was afraid that if I let down my guard for a minute, he would die."

"But he got better."

"And then he relapsed and got better again. His doctors told us that if he passed the five-year mark, the odds were that he'd completely recover. After that second remission, year one passed, and his checkups were good. Then year two. I thought, 'Thank heavens, it's over.' I discovered that if I stayed busy enough, I didn't have time to think about losing my son. That's why I became a realtor and why I worked for Larry. I stayed as busy as I could. But when Adam relapsed this time, I knew it wasn't over. I realized Adam was on loan to us—all children are on loan, you know. You give birth to them, you take care of them, you raise them, but eventually, they leave you. One way or the other."

"College—" Alexis started.

"Or a job, or getting married. That's the natural order of things. Adam's leaving is unnatural. But we can't stop it."

Alexis felt tears sliding down her cheeks. *Unnatural . . .* Her mother had it right.

Eleanor lifted an age-yellowed envelope from between the pages of the baby book. She opened it and removed two thick clusters of light brown hair, one tied with a pink ribbon, the other with a blue one. "These are from your first haircuts. Touch them. Feel how soft."

Mesmerized, Alexis took the hair clippings and cradled them in her palm. They were as soft as down, and in the lamp's light, they shone.

"I love you both so much," Eleanor said, her voice catching. In the silence of the room, a clock ticked. "I know this is crazy, Ally, but the first time Adam got sick, it almost broke our family apart. This time, his illness has brought us back together. Believe it or not, you are responsible for this togetherness, in part. And for that, I will always be grateful."

Tessa wept when Alexis told her what was happening to Adam. They were standing in the parking lot after school. The sky was the color of cornflowers and was decorated with plumes of billowing white clouds. A tropical breeze danced around them. "And he knows?" Tessa asked, wiping her teary eyes.

"He knows."

"So any day now—?"

"Yes. It can happen at any time." Alexis held herself rigid, afraid she'd break down if she didn't.

"Can I . . . Do you think I can visit him more often?"

"I'll ask."

When Alexis asked, Adam shrugged. "I don't know why she'd want to."

"Because she cares," Alexis told him.

"Speaking of caring, I don't see much of Sawyer hanging around here."

"He's busy with soccer."

Adam eyed her skeptically. "Is that all?"

Truthfully, they had never made up after their fight. Alexis figured it was better that way. She missed him, but she didn't have the energy to continually butt heads with him. "As soon as soccer season's over, we'll be tripping over each other," she said. "Just you wait and see." She handed Adam a party bag splashed with the words GET WELL. "By the way . . . Tessa and I made this for you."

He pulled away the tissue and lifted out a dark brown teddy bear. The stuffed toy wore a baseball cap and held a bat emblazoned with the word SLUGGER. It wore a tiny T-shirt marked with the insignia of their school baseball team. On the back of the shirt was a large #1. Adam grinned. "He's cool. Thanks."

"We thought you deserved a bear of your own."

"I should call Tessa up and thank her."

"You should call her up and invite her over and tell her goodbye."

Adam's gaze searched his sister's for a long time. At last he said, "I should have picked her instead of Kelly."

"Yes . . . I've always thought so too. Which is something else you can tell her."

"It's too late now."

"It's never too late, Adam. Not as long as you have breath to say the words."

He reached up his hand. "You're a great sister."

She laced her fingers through his. "And you love me, right?"

"And I love you," he echoed.

Alexis stood outside the door of Mrs. Wiley's room, taking deep breaths to steady her nerves. The halls were empty. She'd waited in the library until the buses had left and the parking lot was devoid of student cars so that she could see Mrs. Wiley privately. She rapped gently on the door.

Mrs. Wiley glanced up from the paperwork

spread across her desk. "Alexis!" She smiled broadly. "Come on in. Sit."

"I—I'm sorry to bother you."

"It's never a bother to see one of my favorite students and captain of the best debate team I've ever coached."

Alexis groaned inwardly. Mrs. Wiley wasn't making this easy. She took another deep breath. "I have to tell you something."

Mrs. Wiley looked expectant.

"Mrs. Wiley, I'm not going to state with you."

The smile faded from the teacher's face. "What?" The team was to leave on Thursday for Tallahassee.

"I—I can't leave," Alexis said. "Adam's too sick. If something happens to him while I'm gone, I won't be able to live with myself."

"Oh, Alexis, I do understand, but we'll only be gone three days. You'll be home Sunday night. And the team's counting on you."

Alexis shook her head. "I just can't go. Maybe nothing will happen to Adam if I go, but I can't take a chance."

Mrs. Wiley slumped in her chair. She looked befuddled. "I—I don't know what to say. You're the team captain. You're our top debater."

"Tessa can do it. She's really better than I am

in a lot of ways. She'll lead the team, and she'll fight to win."

"Of course she's good, but you—"

"Won't be there," Alexis stated firmly.

Mrs. Wiley pursed her lips. "I was going to save this until we arrived at the hotel, but professors from Stetson are coming, at my special request, just to observe you."

Alexis felt her heart squeeze, but still she shook her head. "That was nice of you, but I—I can't."

Mrs. Wiley removed her glasses and pinched the bridge of her nose. She released a deep, weary sigh. "All right, child. I know you well enough to realize you've thought this through, and I shouldn't be putting pressure on you. It's just that we're so good with you on the team. You'll be missed."

Alexis shifted her book bag, knowing that once she walked out the door her high school debating career would be finished. "Thank you. I'd be glad to call everyone on the team and explain." She'd already told Tessa, who hadn't even tried to dissuade her.

Mrs. Wiley said, "No . . . you have enough on your mind. I'll tell the team."

"Tell them that they're very good and that

they can do this with or without me." She turned to leave.

"If you change your mind . . ."

"I won't," Alexis said over her shoulder.

She made it out of the school and into her car in the parking lot before she broke down and cried.

The debate team left Thursday afternoon for the state capital. On Friday morning, Eleanor woke Alexis up. "Hurry, get dressed. Adam's breathing is bad. Your father's called the paramedics and they're on their way."

NINETEEN

At the hospital, Adam was checked in to the ICU and put on a ventilator. "It will help him breathe," the doctor told Alexis and her parents. "But he won't be able to speak with the tube down his throat if he regains consciousness."

"*Will* he wake?" Blake asked.

The doctor's expression was sad. "That's doubtful. His body's pretty well worn out. His liver function is almost nil, and his kidneys are failing too."

Alexis felt the doctor's words in her soul. Adam would not go home again.

"H-how long?" Eleanor's voice trembled, and Blake put his arms around her.

"Hard to say exactly. Maybe twenty-four to forty-eight hours. I wish it didn't have to be this way. I wish we could have helped him."

• • •

Alexis returned to the waiting room where she'd spent the night when they'd first brought Adam to the hospital months before. In the daylight, the room appeared shopworn and dingy. Two other families were hunkered down, awaiting turns to visit their loved ones in the ICU. For Adam's family, there were no time restrictions on their staying with him. They could come and go at will since the end was near.

Alexis found a couch off to one side of the room and sat down to collect her thoughts and tattered emotions. She didn't want to fall apart in Adam's room. A nurse had told them that hearing was the last of the five senses to go for a patient, and Alexis wanted to be strong for Adam's sake.

"Hey, pumpkin. Can I join you?"

She looked up to see her father. "You haven't called me pumpkin since I was six."

"That's when you told me not to call you pumpkin anymore because you were too big and it was a baby name." A little smile crossed his mouth. "You'll always be my pumpkin, you know."

She didn't know what to say, didn't know how to locate that little girl for him again. He looked tired and older than he had ever seemed to her before.

"Do you want anything?" he asked. "Food? Coffee?"

"I want to call Tessa, but I know she's right in the middle of the tournament, and it wouldn't be fair to tell her this now."

"I'm sorry you couldn't be with your team. I know how hard you've worked."

"It doesn't matter. I want to be here." She leaned on his shoulder and he put his arm around her. "Daddy, this is so hard."

"I know," he said. "I'll never have another son." His words stabbed at her heart. "I'm glad I came home for lunch every day this past month. Did Adam tell you?"

Surprised, she shook her head. He had not told her.

"We ate in his room. And we talked. Gave your mother a break too." Blake stroked Alexis's hair. "I'm sorry I didn't take more time to get to know him better sooner."

"Adam understood."

"There's no excuse, Ally. A person can't buy back lost time."

Alexis felt tears well up. Ultimately, Adam's illness had afflicted all of them. Like a destructive moth, it had eaten into the fabric of their family, leaving holes none of them had mended. "For so long, you and Mom were like strangers. I thought you didn't care about us anymore. . . . I was scared."

"Defensive mode," he said. She saw the stubble of his beard on his chin, dark, mixed with gray. "If you don't care, then you can't get hurt. Trouble was, I couldn't not care no matter how hard I tried or how many long hours I worked. Back then, the notions that my son was sick and his doctors weren't sure they could make him well just didn't compute for me. There I was, one of the best-known attorneys in the city. I fixed things for clients. I solved problems for people all the time. But I couldn't fix my own son. The feeling of total helplessness almost did me in, and instead of pulling us all closer, I disappeared into my work. I handled things badly, and I regret that."

Alexis picked at her fingernail polish, then looked up. Her heart began to hammer, and she knew it was time to ask him the question that had been on her mind for months. "Dad . . . I saw you in a restaurant once with another woman. She was blond and young and pretty. I wasn't spying. . . . It just happened."

His face reddened, but he didn't say anything. Alexis squirmed and wondered if she'd stepped too far out of bounds. Maybe it would be better to *not* hear his explanation. She wasn't sure she could endure more bad news.

"Her name is Amy," her father said eventually. "She's a law clerk at the firm—bright, energetic, not unlike you. She looked to me as her mentor, and I was flattered. I took her to dinner twice. But nothing ever happened between us, Ally." He lifted her chin. "Nothing. I have never been unfaithful to your mother. We've had our rough spells, but I've never loved any woman but her. And that's the truth."

Alexis felt relieved, but also embarrassed to have even asked the question. In her eyes, her parents had once been perfect, her father a god, her mother the queen of the world. She saw them now as ordinary people, flawed and desperately trying to find purpose and reason within a darkness too vast to comprehend. A darkness that was about to swallow them all. Her heart hurt and her mind felt numb. Both her parents had come to her with their confessions, and she realized that both wanted absolution from her. She was the one who remained. She was the one who held their shared memories of things done and things left undone. She was their daughter. Their only daughter, and the keeper of their dreams.

He stood. "I should go stay with your mother."

"I'll be there in a minute." She watched him leave, knowing she would wait before going in to give them time together to be with their only son.

Around five in the morning a sense of urgency woke Alexis from a sound sleep. She gathered up her belongings and returned to the ICU room where her parents held vigil over Adam. She dragged a chair alongside theirs, and curling her legs beneath her, she joined their bedside watch. The rails on the bed were up, and she reached through them and put her hand over her brother's to connect them with each other.

By seven o'clock, and with the hospital's shift change, she noticed people drifting into the unit, nurses and caregivers whom she recognized from the oncology floor where Adam had stayed for so long. They came in quietly, touched his motionless body, and left. Often, they had something kind to say, like "Your son was the nicest kid I ever cared for," and "Adam brought so much happiness to the floor. Everybody liked him," and

"He was one in a million. Like a big brother to the little kids." Their words and gestures brought Alexis comfort, and she hoped Adam somehow knew how many people cared about him. He gave no sign that he did know. The ventilator did its job of breathing for him. The monitors kept track of his vital signs.

The end came gently. His heart simply stopped beating. A monitor let off a loud whine that caused them all to jump. A nurse came running. She switched off the machine. The only sound was the hiss of the ventilator. "He's gone," the nurse said.

Gone. Adam's soul, his essence had vanished from their time and space. "Turn off the ventilator," Blake said.

She did, and the air stilled. "You can stay as long as you want," the nurse told them, fighting tears.

Alexis felt a tearing inside her mind, a rending, a sense of aloneless she had never felt before. She could no longer reach through the bed's rails and touch her brother's life. He had gone someplace without her, and only her own death would allow her to meet him again.

Suddenly the room seemed to close in on her, and she could scarcely catch her breath. "I—I'll be down the hall," she mumbled, and left on wobbly legs.

Outside the unit, the air felt cooler, less suffocating. She put her hand on the wall to steady herself, looked up. The hall was dimly lit, but she saw someone standing down by the elevator. He was backlit, but there was no mistaking the tall, square shape, the tousled hair. She broke into a run, and Sawyer opened his arms. She threw herself against him, sobbing. "Adam died."

"I'm sorry, baby. So sorry about everything. Please forgive me."

"H-how did you—?"

"Tessa told me you weren't going to state. When I got home from school, I called you and I kept calling, but there was no answer. I finally figured out where you must be, so I came."

His arms closed around her, and she clung to him. He was her anchor in this sea of agony. He was her safe haven, and for the moment, he was her home.

TWENTY

On graduation day at the Miami-Dade Civic Center, in a class of 513 seniors walking two by two, Alexis Chappel walked alone. Dressed in a navy blue cap and gown, she carried a single long-stemmed white rose. Tessa, Glory and Charmaine had given it to her in the staging area to carry in Adam's memory. The graduation program offered a brief paragraph about losing Adam to cancer, which the principal read from the podium. When her name was called, Alexis walked across the stage and took her certificate from Mrs. Wiley, who shook her hand and beamed her a congratulatory smile. The debate team had finished second in the state tournament, but it was losing only two seniors—Alexis and Tessa—and there was always next year.

Her parents took her to dinner afterward. She

told Tessa and Sawyer that she'd meet them at the graduation party at Charmaine's house later. All through the meal, the empty space at the restaurant table for four seemed especially poignant. No one mentioned it.

When dessert was served—crème brûlée; her favorite—her father handed her a gift bag and placed a large, heavy manila envelope on the table. "The goodie bag's from me and your mother."

Alexis removed a small velvet box, raised the lid and discovered an exquisite pair of diamond stud earrings. "Oh my gosh! They're beautiful!"

"There's a bracelet that goes with them when you graduate from college, and a necklace when you've passed the bar," her father said.

"You'll spoil the surprise," Eleanor chided.

"Sounds like bribery to me," Alexis said.

"So call a cop," her father joked. "Turn me in." He slid the envelope toward her. "This came last week, but we saved it for you to open today."

Alexis saw that the return address was Stetson University, Office of Admissions. Her heart raced. "A rejection letter wouldn't come in an envelope this big, would it?"

"Open it and see," Eleanor said.

Alexis tore open the packet. Her letter of acceptance was on top. She waved it at her parents. "I'm in!" The other material consisted of financial and housing forms, booklets and pamphlets. "There's so much *stuff*!"

"Congratulations," her mother said.

Alexis hugged the sheaf of papers to her. "I thought I'd blown it. I thought that because I didn't go to state, they wouldn't consider me."

"I guess you were wrong," her father said.

She looked from one parent to the other. They looked happy. She hadn't thought they'd ever smile again, but now they were smiling, and they looked proud of her. And she was proud of them. They had joined Candle Lighters, a support group for parents who had lost children to cancer. There was a teen support group too, which Alexis was planning to attend. The loss of Adam was fresh and painful, but no amount of tears could bring him back to them. They all had to learn the new math for their family. The four of them had turned into three, and the three would turn to two when Alexis moved away to college.

"We have one other announcement to make," her mother said.

"I'm listening."

"Your father and I are setting up a foundation in Adam's name. Your dad's doing the paperwork, I'm doing the fund-raising. The goal is to make sure every child who enters a Miami hospital, for whatever reason, gets a brand-new teddy bear to cuddle. We're calling the foundation Adam's Boo-Boo Bears. A kid's age won't matter, because as you once told us, you're never too old for a teddy bear."

Tears welled in Alexis's eyes. "Never," she said, remembering the day they'd all worked on Adam's Christmas project.

Her mother leaned forward, her expression one of eager determination. "I have big plans for the foundation. We'll raise money to buy toys and other things for the pediatric floors that the hospital can't afford. We're even thinking about doing Christmas baskets and throwing parties every time a child completes chemo. What do you think?"

If anyone could pull off such a grand plan, it would be her mother. "I think Adam would be pleased," Alexis said.

"You helped make it happen, you know. You made a difference, Ally, and we want you to be a part of it. Your ideas are welcome."

"If I have any, I'll let you know," she said.

"When I'm not studying to earn that diamond bracelet."

Both of her parents laughed, and the sound flowed through her like an electric current, radiating warmth to the depths of her heart.

Sawyer came over to her house a week later, waving a letter and grinning broadly. "My scholarship to Duke came through."

"Way to go," Alexis said, giving him a hug. She was pleased for him because it was something he'd wanted for so long. Duke University had an NCAA soccer team that was one of the best in the country.

"I'll ride the bench for the first year, but that's okay. I'll have top coaching, and I'll play with some of the best talent in the country. Aside from myself, that is."

She rolled her eyes.

He said, "I've been looking over the schedule for the season. We play a tournament in Orlando in the fall. And that means you can come be with me." Deland, where Stetson was, wasn't that far from Orlando. "Then for spring break, I figure we can both head over to Daytona Beach. What do you think?" His blue eyes grew serious.

"Spring is a long way off. You know, you may

find a girl at Duke you'll want to date." She didn't want to lock him into a commitment he might regret later.

"You're the girl I want," he said.

"But just maybe—"

He pressed his fingertips to her lips. "Are you trying to dump me?"

She shook her head. "Your feelings could change."

"Impossible."

She slipped her arms around his neck. "All right. Let's see how it goes. Just remember, I have the ability to read minds."

He pulled back, grinned. "Then read this," he said, and he kissed her.

Alexis felt she had one piece of unfinished business left before she could head off to college. She chose a warm summer day when she was alone in the house and when she knew she wouldn't be interrupted. She'd been thinking about doing it for a long time, and now the timing seemed perfect.

She found a large box in the garage and dragged it upstairs. She paused briefly at the closed door of Adam's room, took a deep breath, opened the door and walked in. The room was pristine, with every item in its place and the scents of lemon wax and freshly washed linen saturating the air. The cleaning woman had done up the room the week after Adam's death, but Alexis saw him everywhere—on his bed, by his closet, at his desk. She knew that her parents sometimes slipped inside to sit on the bed and soak up what remained of their son. It was something they'd learned at their support group meetings. *Grieving takes time. Don't rush it.*

Alexis didn't know how long they would leave the room intact; that would be up to her mother and father. She only knew what she had to do for *her* sake. She was going to gather up some of Adam's things and create a time capsule of her own. She planned to tuck it away, just as Ms. Lola had saved the papers from their first-grade class; then one day, perhaps when she was grown, or married, or a mother herself, she would open it up and revisit the brother she had loved and lost.

She picked up his baseball. The well-worn hide was smudged, but she held it along the stitching the way she'd often seen him do. She thumped it once against the wall behind the door, and the familiar, solid thud made her smile. She went through his dresser, found a sweatshirt that still held his scent. She buried her nose in the fabric, fought the urge to cry and dropped it into the box with the baseball. She combed the room methodically, choosing from his favorite comic books, his baseball trophies, his Matchbox car collection. She tossed in several of his school notebooks and a few important photographs from an old box where he had stashed them along with the negatives.

She removed the thumbtack that held his first-grade wish to his bulletin board. She traced her fingers over the childish block letters—*I want to be a fireman.*

Some dreams don't come true, she thought.

Alexis knew she had a letter to write and went to her room to compose it.

Dear Ms. Lola:

I'm heading off to college next week, but I can't leave without writing you and telling you how I feel. First of all, I want to thank you for being such a great teacher. If you hadn't given me such a good start, I might never have liked school as much as I did. You made learning fun and interesting—even math! I'm telling you this

*because I don't think kids say thank you enough
to the teachers who make a difference in their
lives.*

*I also want to thank you for visiting Adam
in the hospital when he was sick. It meant a lot
to him to know that someone besides his family
was thinking about him. Adam had a terrible
crush on you way back then, and always called you
a little elf.*

*Thank you also for the time capsule you kept.
And for the ceremony inviting us back to hear all our
kid wishes. I didn't know at the time that it would be
the last school ceremony I ever attended with my
brother. I'm still sad whenever I think about how
Adam's life was cut so short, but I make myself concentrate on the good and not the bad, and that helps
me keep control.*

*Most of all, I want to thank you for the whole
time capsule idea. I liked it so much that I have cre-
ated my own time capsule dedicated to Adam's memory. I'm saving many of his things, and I know that
someday, when I'm much stronger, I will be able to
open it and touch my brother again. I will be able to
use it to show my future friends and my future family (if I get married and have kids!) all about Adam
too, for I know the things I'm saving will help him
become real to them. He deserves that, I think.*

Ms. Lola, I will never forget your influence on my life. I will never forget your thoughtfulness and kindness. The first graders of tomorrow will be lucky to have you for their teacher. Think of me now and again. Think of Adam too.

Your grateful student,

Alexis Chappel

———————— ⟲ ————————

"I miss you . . . ," she whispered to Adam when she finished writing. She and Adam, tucked so compactly beneath their mother's heart inside the dark, warm comfort of the womb. They had been two halves, made whole by each other's existence. Now she felt split in two again, cleaved, as if some great knife had sliced them apart. Holding the letter, she returned to Adam's room.

Don't be sad. The words formed like a whisper inside her mind, as if he'd spoken them aloud. "You're here, aren't you, Adam?" She heard no answer, but it didn't matter. She didn't have to see the sun to know it existed. Adam's room was alive, all but vibrating with his essence. The presence she felt was no illusion.

She lifted the box, rested it on her hip, took another long, searching look around the room, opened the door to the hall. Adam was with her. Not in his possessions, but in her mind, in her memory. She would keep him alive inside the time capsule of her heart. Always.

MAKE YOUR OWN TIME CAPSULE

Maybe you'd like to create a time capsule for yourself. It's fun and easy, and if you do it correctly, your keepsakes can last a long, long time. According to the International Time Capsule Society, here's how to do it.

1. *Choose a container.* It can be plastic, metal, or heavy-duty rubber—as long as it's nonbiodegradable and airtight. Coffee cans work great, but you may want to use something larger.

2. *Choose a date.* Decide when you (or future generations!) will open your time capsule. After you graduate from college? In ten years? Twenty? Fifty? Write that date on a large adhesive label: DO NOT OPEN UNTIL _____; then stick it on your container.

3. *Choose your contents.* What do you want to put in your time capsule? Use your imagination. Fill

your container with things that represent both world events and what's going on in your life right now. Clip headlines from newspapers and magazines. Since newsprint is fragile, photocopy news articles onto archival-quality paper, which can be found at your local craft or hobby store.

You can also add photos of yourself, your family, your pets and your friends. Wrap photographs in archival-quality envelopes to protect them, and be sure to label them so you'll remember who's in them, where you were and what you were doing.

Be creative! Add ticket stubs from movies and plays and programs from events you attended. Include CDs or CD-ROMs of your favorite music or computer games. Why not write a letter to your future self or to the people who will open your time capsule? Write about your everyday life, your feelings, your hopes and dreams. Be sure to use acid-free paper so that your words will stand the test of time. Your local craft store's scrapbook or stamping department usually stocks this kind of writing paper.

4. *Get other people involved.* Invite family and friends to contribute to your time capsule. To preserve items that aren't papers or photographs, seal each in a plastic bag, and label it so that you know where it came from.

5. *Seal it!* Now it's time to seal your time capsule, so gather all the items, put them in a large plastic bag for extra protection and put that bag into your container. Make sure the lid fits tightly. If necessary, seal it with duct tape or glue.

6. *Hide it!* Even though a lot of people bury their time capsules, it isn't a good idea. You might forget where you buried your capsule, or you might move. Many time capsules have been lost this way. Instead, pick a location that's cool, dark and dry—this will ensure that the things you've put in your capsule will last for a long time. Think about shoving it to the back of your closet, locking it in a drawer or even storing it in plain sight on a shelf in your room. (No peeking!)

7. *Leave yourself a reminder.* If you've hidden your time capsule, write a note to remind yourself when to open it. Leave the note in a place where you're sure to find it—your desk drawer, your diary, a home file cabinet.

8. *Open it!* In the future, that is! You're going to love meeting yourself years from now. And you'll be surprised at the amazing memories when you do.

ABOUT THE AUTHOR

Lurlene McDaniel began writing inspirational novels about teenagers facing life-altering situations when her son was diagnosed with juvenile diabetes. "I saw firsthand how chronic illness affects every aspect of a person's life," she has said. "I want kids to know that while people don't get to choose what life gives to them, they do get to choose how they respond."

Lurlene McDaniel's novels are hard-hitting and realistic, but also leave readers with inspiration and hope. Her books have received acclaim from readers, teachers, parents and reviewers. Her novel *Angels Watching Over Me* and its companions, *Lifted Up by Angels* and *Until Angels Close My Eyes*, have all been national bestsellers, as have *Don't Die, My Love*; *I'll Be Seeing You*; and *Till Death Do Us Part*. *Six Months to Live* was included in a literary time capsule at the Library of Congress in Washington, D.C.

Lurlene McDaniel lives in Chattanooga, Tennessee.